A HERO'S CHRISTMAS KISS

GREEN HILLS BOOK 8

A MILITARY KISSES SWEET ROMANCE

VIRGINIA'DELE SMITH

Published by Books are Ubiquitous, Inc.
in the United States of America
booksareubiquitous.com

Books are Ubiquitous is a federally
registered trademark.

This book is a work of fiction.

Names, characters, places, and incidents either are the product of the author's imagination or are used fictitiously. Any resemblance to actual persons, living or dead, business establishments, events, or locales is entirely coincidental.

PAPERBACK ISBN 978-1-957036-33-5

———

Titles by Virginia'dele Smith

Sadie & Sam: PART 1 - Introductory Short Story (FREE)
Book 0: My Manifesto - Short Memoir (FREE)

THE MILITARY KISSES COLLECTION

**The *Military Kisses* collection
is a multi-author series
of 20 heartwarming clean romance stories
filled with all the cozy, small-town
charm you love…
with a military twist.**

*E*nough holiday to cheer to keep you warm all throughout the season!

When these heroes and heroines agree to come for the holidays, they never expected to find *forever* waiting under the Christmas tree.

———

***The Military Kisses Sweet Romance series
is available on Amazon.***

*To all the military heroes
and the people who love them.*

1

Too busy to take notice when the bell above Brew's door jingled, Emilie Fielding wiped a cleaning rag across the counter in front of the only empty stool at the bar, flipped a thick ceramic mug, and poured a steaming cup of coffee with practiced ease. She'd replaced the pot on the burner, pulled orders for two tables from the kitchen pass-through, and shimmied past the coffee shop's newest guest without glancing up to see who'd arrived. As she served plates to both tables at once, shushed silence descended upon the tiny dining room. That got Emilie's attention.

Her eyes danced over the patrons, all regulars who practically lived in Brew and never stopped talking. Emilie followed their gazes — every single one — to the no-longer-empty spot at the bar and settled on a broad back, covered in a midnight-navy fleece vest hunched over the cup of coffee she'd just poured. Under the vest, the man — because with a build like that, he was most definitely a stout and strong *man* — wore a gray-and-blue, buffalo-checked flannel shirt with the sleeves rolled up to reveal tanned, sinewy forearms, apparently too hot-blooded to be bothered by the freezing temperatures torturing Green Hills on the first day of December. By contrast, he'd wrapped both his large hands around the warm cup, as though welcoming its heat. Long legs encased in heavy, charcoal-gray hunting pants led to a pair of black military-issue boots, which he'd propped on the footrail attached to the ancient coffee counter. He looked relaxed, but one foot bounced in a staccato rhythm.

Like a preschool teacher reprimanding her recalcitrant students, Emilie cast disapproving frowns as she finished handing out plates, silently pointing everyone's attention back to their own business as she wound her way behind the counter. She replaced her reprimanding glower with a neutral smile and waited for conversations to resume before approaching the newcomer.

As she refilled the stranger's coffee, the bell above the door jingled again, and a cluster of teenagers shuffled indoors. They piled into a booth with friends, happy to sit like sardines wedged in a can.

"Heaven sure has been busy today," Emilie mumbled under her breath. In one smooth motion, she again returned the coffeepot to its burner, snagged a round serving tray, and began putting ice into glasses with the metal scoop in her right hand while using the left to fill each glass with water. Then, reminiscent of a casino dealer handling a deck of cards, her fingers flew, cutting small slits in lemon wheels and hanging them on the glasses' rims before loading the tray. Emilie hefted it onto her shoulder and grabbed a stack of menus.

"Is this heaven?"

The question, voiced in a deep, almost raspy voice, stopped Emilie midmotion.

She turned back to find the stranger studying his mug. Emilie knew he'd been the one to speak, but he seemed disinclined to say more. She tucked the menus under her arm, lowered the tray of drinks back onto the counter, and did some studying of her own.

Her gaze traveled along the muscled forearms, up a rigid, straight neck, and across well-defined cheeks covered in a close-cropped beard. His hair, cut in a military fade that had grown a little long on top, resembled honey — smooth and rich and golden-blond. It was darker than her own long tresses, butter-blonde and straight-as-a-board, which Emilie often bemoaned for being flat and boring.

His head lifted. Their eyes met. The haunting intensity in his sent a chill down Emilie's spine, not from fear of him, but fear *for* him…for what caused such volatility. Her heart went out to him.

And luckily, she regained her senses.

"Sorry," she said, shaking off the daze and offering a gentle, apologetic smile. "No," she added with a chuckle. "Definitely not heaven, but about as close as you'll find. Green Hills, I mean," she added, quick to correct herself. "*Not* Brew." She lifted an eyebrow in playful exasperation. "This place is more like a circus, complete with a troupe of clowns who love to mess with my day." Despite the truth she spoke about the unruly band of retirees across the room, Emilie smiled at their table with adoring fondness.

"Do they come here often?" her newcomer asked, his voice still low and raw.

"Every single day," Emilie confirmed. "I've convinced them to give me thirty minutes in the mornings, just to get the lights turned on and the coffee started, so they trickle in around 7:30, and I kick them out at 3:30 to clean and close up by 4:30. Then we do it all over again the next day."

"So, this *is* their heaven."

"More like their headquarters. From that table right there, they plot the lives of poor, unsuspecting innocents, worry over the future, and replay days of old — with varying degrees of fact versus fantasy."

"Sounds like heaven to me," the man said. The directness with which his gaze bore into Emilie sent another tingle across her skin.

Unable to find the right words, she agreed with a small nod.

"Miss Em," a perky girl at the teens' table called out. "Are there any muffins left from breakfast?"

"I'd better take these over and feed the kids before they turn into monsters," Emilie teased, balancing the tray of water glasses on her palm and shoulder. She tossed another smile at the stranger before walking away, hoping he recognized the welcome and friendliness she'd hoped to impart.

When she returned to the coffee counter, he was gone.

No name. No explanation of what brought him to Brew, or even through Green Hills.

Emilie knew absolutely nothing about their quiet visitor, and yet she wouldn't soon forget him.

Not how soft his lips looked, nor the worry on his brow. Not the rumble of his voice, nor his powerful presence.

Just the thought of the man brought a flush to her checks.

When Emilie moved to gather his napkin and empty coffee cup, she couldn't help but smile...

Beside his mug rested an origami angel, made from a ten-dollar bill.

2

*Every great athlete, artist and aspiring being
has a great team to help them flourish and succeed —
personally and professionally.*
Rasheed Ogunlaru

"Dr. Ramon, is that a new Christmas sweater?" Emilie asked the next morning, *oohing* and *ahhing* over the physician who'd delivered her twenty-eight years earlier — and most every baby born in Green Hills between about 1965 and his official retirement five years ago.

"It is," he confirmed, holding out the knit waistband to flatten the holiday scene for a better look. The elaborate design featured nine reindeer pulling Santa in his sleigh, flying across a midnight sky filled with stars — silver sequins — twinkling over a row of festively decorated shops along a snowy street. A red, battery-operated bulb flashed, lighting Rudolph's nose.

"Wow," Emilie stated, dumbfounded and forced to flatten her lips in a tight line to suppress her giggle.

"It's a lot," Alden Ramon replied, bug-eyed with bewilderment. "But you know, whatever the great-grandkids pick out, this old Poppa is happy to wear. They'll be by to pick me up in a while for family phot—"

"Coffee's tepid," Mr. Moody complained, interrupting and speaking over Doc, right before blowing on his mug to test the temperature with a tiny sip. Emilie mouthed *Sorry!* to Dr. Ramon.

"Nah," Ms. Cheyenne countered, waving off Alfred Moody's grumpiness while inhaling the potent scent of freshly brewed coffee. "It's perfect," she added before indulging in her first drink.

"Thank you," Emilie answered with a conspiratorial wink at the stunning Native American woman whose words meant more because she rarely spoke them, usually content to listen and absorb the world around her. Then Emilie set an extra-large mug in front of the man to the right of Ms. Cheyenne. "I added a shot of honey and a blend of cinnamon and ginger to yours, Mr. Sneed. It might taste a little sweeter than usual, but I want you to kick this allergy that keeps hanging around."

"What would we do without— *Achooo!*" A wracking sneeze cut off the sweet old man who seemed to fight a tickle in his throat every time the wind blew. "You take such good care of us," he concluded after blowing his nose on an old-fashioned handkerchief, one of a countless stash his late wife embroidered decades ago, and which were never far from his pocket.

"I hope you added an extra shot of caffeine to mine," Alora Johnson groaned on the heels of a yawn as she reached out for a cup from Emilie.

"*If* we had an espresso machine, I'd be happy to fix you right up," Emilie replied, sending a pointed look at Mr. Moody, Brew's proprietor and Emilie's boss, who merely pursed his lips in response.

"I think that sounds lovely," Blythe Asher said, her voice a light, effervescent song. "What do you think, Obie?" She and Emilie looked to the final member of the group, both wearing warm smiles for their beloved friend — Mr. Obadiah Bernard III —who made a dramatic show of mulling over the matter before nodding excitedly in affirmation. His eyes held humor, and his shoulders shook with silent laughter.

In 1973, after boot camp and one thirteen-month rotation with the US Marine Sub Unit One, which was a specialized unit of the 1st Air Naval Gunfire Liaison Company known as ANGLICO that provided fire support and target coordination for Marine and allied forces during the Vietnam War, the nineteen-year-old who'd enlisted to serve his country the day he turned eighteen, returned home. The war hadn't claimed his life, like so many of his comrades, but it had claimed his voice. Whether his muteness resulted from an injury or nerves or sights he could never unsee, no one in Green Hills knew for sure. No matter the cause, Obadiah — better known by his childhood nickname, Obie — hadn't uttered a word in nearly fifty years.

His lack of speech hadn't made Obie weak, though. To the contrary, his resilience, patience, and dependability took center stage at the Green Hills Country Club, where Obie spent forty-five years as the course superintendent. He had not only overseen the grounds and maintenance, transforming a quaint and somewhat outdated golf facility into 200 acres of picturesque, tree-lined fairways, immaculate greens, and enough challenges to make it a fun course for players of all skill levels. During his tenure, the country club caught the eye of professionals, who enjoyed practicing there between tournaments. Glowing word-of-mouth reviews translated into GHCC hosting a regional PGA Junior League tournament, which led to an LPGA event for women, and then to an annual charity golf weekend with the All Pro Tour. Obie's vision for the club, his work ethic, and his dedication to excellence had benefited Green Hills in profound ways. There was no telling the economic impact to date, and no way to imagine future rewards. At first glance, one might see a mute yet jovial man when looking at Obie, but if they took the time to get to know him, they'd discover someone truly brilliant and vastly accomplished underneath his almost childlike demeanor.

Emilie squeezed Obie's shoulder with affection and finished filling their mugs. Then she returned to her counter for a platter of donuts, fresh fruit, and sizzling bacon waiting in the order-up window. The bell above the door rang as she placed the breakfast goodies on the table, within easy reach of her seven super seniors.

Here we go, she thought, fully expecting another harried day on her feet. The deep fryer wasn't reaching full temperature, the lightbulb in the walk-in refrigerator needed replacing, she'd received a call that the linen service was running late, and the dining room needed decorating. She exhaled a deep breath, blowing stray strands of hair from her eyes. She could cement her ponytail with hairspray, and five minutes later, the fine strands would tickle her eyelashes. *Harrumph!*

"That was great coffee yesterday; mind if I get another cup?"

The husky voice rattled Emilie. She'd prayed she'd hear it again, but she hadn't truly believed she would.

Brushing the flyaways from her eyes, Emilie tried to look relaxed and normal when she turned to face the handsome stranger.

But is he a stranger? I met him yesterday. I certainly didn't forget him. Or his commanding presence. I'd recognize him if I saw him out. Yeah…I mean, I know him. Sort of…

Emilie shook the meandering thoughts from her mind as he settled onto the same stool where he'd sat the day before. She set a coffee cup in front of him, grabbed the pot, and filled his mug, same as she'd done a million times in the six years she'd been working full time at Brew, not to mention the years she'd worked there part time during high school. So why were her hands less than steady?

After returning the coffeepot to the burner behind her, Emilie turned back to face the mystery man.

"How about some breakfast to go with the coffee today?" She was pleased to hear she sounded as though she had full control over her faculties, even if her heart raced, hoping he'd say yes.

"That'd be nice," he answered. "Anything'll be great."

That was it? *Anything?*

"Oh. Uh, okay. I'll be right back," she told him before dashing into the kitchen.

While Emilie managed the coffee shop for Mr. Moody, overseeing operations while working the counter and serving food, Byron Watts ruled the kitchen. A romantic at heart who loved to wax poetic and philosophize about the meaning of life, his mastery and fierce ownership over the grill, the prep station, the cooktop, the ovens, the freezer, the fridge, and all the ingredients found in any of those locations had earned him the nickname *Lord* Byron.

"Why are you in here?" he demanded the moment Emilie cleared the swing door.

"I need breakfast," she answered, a deer in headlights.

"So write the order on the notepad, tear off the top sheet, and attach it to the order wheel…from *your* side of that wall." Byron pointed at the wall behind Emilie with a metal spatula and an unwavering eye.

"But there's no order," she marveled.

"Then there's no breakfast," he countered.

"I want it all," she stated.

"Excuse me?" he asked.

"Breakfast is the most important meal of the day, right?" Emilie mused, pacing between the dining room wall and the prep island, distracted but still coherent enough not to walk any further into the room. "And he looks like he could use a good meal."

"Who?" Byron's unwavering gaze switched to a questioning one.

"Him."

"Him who?" he tried again.

"The man."

"The man," Byron repeated.

"Yes."

"And what did the man order?"

"He didn't."

"Emilie," Byron growled.

She responded with a wide-eyed look of innocence.

"What did the man *say?*" Byron tried again.

"*Anything'll be great,*" she quoted.

"Anything?"

"Anything," Emilie confirmed with one firm nod. "And so, we'll give him *everything*."

3

*E*milie reemerged from the kitchen to discover a full dining room. She bustled from table to table, delivering waters, taking orders, serving pastries, filling and refilling cups of coffee, and listening for the bell to announce the *everything breakfast* was ready. Finally, Byron rang.

Ditching a table midway through a round of topping off mugs, Emilie dashed for the window, eager to please and wanting his food to arrive piping hot — she really needed to ask his name, or at the very least, make up one for him. *Mmm? Maybe Fabio.* Emilie darted a quick glance at the man in question. *No, he's got nice hair, but not enough to pull off a Fabio. Hemsworth? Now there's a hot name for a hot guy. But that one's already taken, three times over.* She picked up his order from the pass-through. *How about Phoenix?* She turned from the window to face him, analyzing his phoenix-esque. *It works. I could see him rising from the ashes, forged by fire…tested but never defea—*

"Thank you." His deep voice jostled Emilie from her musings. Her eyes volleyed from his fine face to one plate piled high with bacon, scrambled eggs, sausage, and potatoes; to a second plate stacked with three enormous pancakes, decorated with pats of melting butter, drowning in syrup, and sprinkled with powdered sugar; and back to the hopefully starving strang — No, *not* stranger.

"Do you have a name?" Emilie asked, proving she wasn't nearly as in control of her brain as she'd originally believed.

A smile tugged at the corner of his mouth, almost reaching his pretty brown eyes.

An impatient *clang clang clang* from the order bell broke the moment, alerting Emilie to a third plate, filled with two over-sized, fluffy buttermilk biscuits and a soup bowl full of gravy.

"Okay, okay," she laughed, shooting Byron a knowing look. Without meeting Phoenix's gaze, Emilie served his first two plates, brought over the third, and added a glass of orange juice to go with the feast. With that accomplished, she grabbed a rag and a bottle of cleaning spray. Emilie wiped down the counter with gusto and looked *anywhere* except in his direction, desperate to busy herself with *anything*.

"Garrett," Phoenix said while slicing the stack of pancakes.

Emilie paused.

"Pardon?" She looked at him, confused.

"My name is Garrett — Garrett Banks."

"Are you sure?"

He half chuckled, and she grimaced, realizing what she'd asked.

"It's just that—" she began to say.

"I'm sure," he said with humor. Then Phoen— *Garrett* took a bite of his breakfast, set down the fork, and pulled a chain from under his shirt. Dog tags.

"You're a soldier." Emilie's observance fell somewhere between a bewildered question and a sympathetic statement.

That shouldn't have surprised her. Alpha male, in control, take charge, uber strong, athletic-ness oozed off him. *Garrett.*

It fit…sounded courageous and significant. He seemed like a very significant someone.

"For the moment," he commented. His tone had lost its luster. The light in his eyes had flattened. Possibly better to step around that potential land mine.

"Can I ask what brought you to Green Hills? It's a treasure, to be sure, but more of a hidden one," she offered with a smile she hoped would encourage him to keep talking.

"I know a Marine from here—"

"Matty?" Emilie interrupted.

"Gunnery Sergeant Matthias Noble."

"*Aww.* Matty. We miss him so much. I mean, he's not—"

Her stomach dropped. She couldn't say the word out loud.

"No, no," Garrett assured. "He's alive and well, still serving in a MARSOC unit."

"Oh, good," she exclaimed, exhaling with relief. "I'm a few years older than Matty, but Green Hills is tiny, so everyone knows everyone around here. And Matty was quite the athlete, which brings instant celebrity in a small town," she added with a laugh. "He left the day after his high school graduation, and we haven't seen him since. Word trickled back somehow that he'd joined the Marines, but that's all I knew. I'm so glad he's doing well. I knew he would, no matter what he pursued, but hearing it is a treat. Thank you."

Garrett held her gaze for a long moment, as though soaking up her words, like nothing existed beyond their conversation. His directness caused a flutter in her chest. He was just so…much. *Whew.*

"Please, keep eating," Emilie encouraged with a tip of her head toward his waiting breakfast. "While it's hot."

He nodded, either to say you're welcome for the news about Matty, or perhaps just agreeing to resume his meal.

Something about his quiet deliberation made every action mean more, like he thought through every moment and only the important stuff was worth his energy. Emilie had never encountered someone quite like that. He impressed her.

"We went through Raider training together," Garrett said after finishing the pancakes and moving on to the meats and potatoes and eggs. Emilie had begun rolling silverware in cloth napkins — a point of contention with Mr. Moody, who'd adamantly demanded they stick to disposable paper napkins after his wife passed. But Emilie and Roanna had often talked about sprucing up the place with style and class; Emilie saw the pretty floral fabric napkins as a way to honor Mrs. Moody's memory and had refused to acquiesce to Mr. Moody's grumpy demand. When Garrett spoke, she slid her pile of napkins and bin of clean flatware closer to where he sat at the counter and lifted an eyebrow in genuine interest so he'd continue.

"A&S was the toughest," he said.

"A&S?" she asked.

"Assessment & Selection: a grueling test and evaluation of physical and mental strength. Phase 1 was the most challenging time of my life— at least, at the time it was."

"You and Matty went through it together?"

Garrett nodded while finishing a bite. "He talked about Green Hills every night, telling us stories about the people and the places he'd left behind. His tales had us laughing, crying… sometimes simultaneously," he joked with a half-smile. "The image he painted in our minds got a bunch of us through those first three weeks. It sounded too magical to be real, but he promised it was true. *Just off the Indian Nation Turnpike in southeast Oklahoma*, he'd say. And if he said it once, he repeated it a hundred times. I—" He stopped mid-thought. Garrett's chest deflated, his shoulders relaxed. A sad veil dropped over his features. The light disappeared from his eyes again. "Well, I had a little leave coming, so I thought I'd check it out for myself."

"You picked the perfect time," Emilie said with animation, determined to lift his spirits and coax that half-smile back in place. "Christmas in Green Hills is more than a vacation. It's an experience!"

"It would be if we had any decorations up," Mr. Moody offered from across the dining room, nice and loud with a heavy dose of his Scrooge-like cantankerousness.

Emilie offered a patient smile. She rolled the napkin in her hand, set it in a basket of finished silverware bundles, and lifted a fresh pot of coffee with each hand. "I'll be back," she said with a conspiratorial smile while filling his mug. Then she made a round through the dining room, checking on guests, chatting about this and asking about that, while wending her way to the corner table, which housed her seven best customers.

She purposefully ignored Mr. Moody while engaging with everyone *else* in the coffee shop, saving his empty cup for last… when both pots were practically empty.

"Oh, I'm sorry," she declared in a genuine yet sugarcoated voice. "I'm all out. Let me get another pot started," she promised. "You sit tight, Mr. Moody, and I'll be back when it brews…in about fifteen minutes." She cast an innocent smile at the grouchy old man before sashaying away.

"She did that on purpose," he grumbled.

"Of course she did," Doc agreed, chuckling at his old codger of a best friend.

"If you'd buy her that fancy setup she's always talking about, I bet you'd never run out of coffee around here," Blythe added. "And think of all the fancy coffees we could try." Her eyes glittered, and her eyebrows waggled.

"Like rich, strong espressos," Alora added in a dreamy, singsong voice.

"With adorable foam hearts on top," Cheyenne chimed in.

Obie agreed with animated nods, and Mr. Sneed blew his nose yet again.

"Black coffee's all you need," Mr. Moody protested. "Put some cream and sugar in it if you're determined to fancy it up."

"Now, Alfy," Blythe began. "It's not the same, and you know it."

"Don't *Now, Alfy* me," Mr. Moody argued. "That blasted machine Em wants costs over ten thousand dollars! And takes up half the counter space. What do we need with something like that?"

"It's not about the coffee maker," Doc said, ever the wise sage. "Emilie has worked here since high school, came right back when she finished college, and kept the place afloat while Roanna was sick. In the last five years, she's become the heart and soul of Brew. And I know you'd hate to lose her." He spoke his last words in a gentle tone, but they were a firm nudge, all the same.

"*Bah humbug,*" Mr. Moody replied, deepening his permanent frown.

Emilie pretended not to listen as she cleared plates from tables, but she heard every word. And they hit a tender spot in her heart. She didn't want to leave Brew, but she couldn't stay in her current role forever. She had ideas for the coffee shop, financial goals for her future, and dreams of becoming a business owner and entrepreneur. Emilie had put them on the back burner for five years, happy to gain experience while loving life in her sweet hometown. But Green Hills couldn't support more than a couple of hot-beverage bars. With Brew and Steep, the tearoom in town, there wasn't enough foot traffic to warrant a third spot. Opening one would likely force Brew out of business. Emilie would sooner stab herself in the heart than see Roanna Moody's precious shop shut its doors.

Bah humbug was right.

Emilie needed to lift her spirits, too. No better way to do that than to tackle her Christmas to-do list, which started with decorating the coffee shop. And with most of the morning rush heading out for the day, there was no time like the present.

After cleaning and setting the tables, except for the one seven-top in the back of course, Emilie went to check on her soldier. Not *her* soldier…*Garrett*. Merely a Freudian slip.

He was temporary, drifting through on leave. And while Emilie couldn't seem to get him off her mind, he'd given no indication — like, zero signs — that Emilie might be on *his* mind. In fact, he hadn't even asked her name.

That she could rectify.

"I'm Emilie," she announced, standing before him with the coffee counter between them. "Emilie Fielding," she said as she gathered his plates — his completely cleared plates. How in the world had he finished all that food? "Did you get enough to eat?"

Garrett chuckled. Just a soft laugh. The sound did funny things to her stomach.

Oh dear.

"I did," he answered. The little half-grin thing was back. And that did funny things to her nerves.

Lord, please, she prayed, although she did not know what she was asking for. Maybe sanity?

"Oh, well, that's good," she said with a cheerful smile. "Do you have plans for the day?"

"No," he admitted with a self-effacing grimace. He half stood from his stool and rubbed a hand on the back of his neck. "I saw a bookstore down the street and thought I might stop in for something to read."

"It doesn't open until later this afternoon," Emilie explained. "But it's wonderful, so definitely stop by before you leave town," she added.

"Yeah, I will," he said, obviously unsure what to do next.

"If you're free for a while, I could use some help." Where had *that* come from?

His body language screams "ready to bolt." So naturally, you should put him on the spot to stay. Good grief!

"I mean, I could use a second set of hands hanging Christmas lights and greenery around the shop, if you're looking for something to do. It's manual labor," she joked, "but I can pay you in homemade pumpkin, pecan, or buttermilk chess pie."

A dark shadow drifted over Garrett's face but floated away as quickly as it had appeared. Had she said something wrong?

"But please don't feel obligated," Emilie gushed. "There are so many more exciting things to do in Green Hills! You could drive out to Daisy Lake, fish at the marina, hike the lake trail, or take a boat out. Or you could—"

"I'm happy to help," Garrett said, interrupting, but with an indulgent smile. One click up from the half-smile…moving in the right direction.

Emilie smiled back. She'd done that quite a bit in the brief minutes she'd been in his company.

And she was determined to return the favor.

That moment decided it: Making this enigmatic, and admittedly, *smoking hot* man smile — really smile — became her Christmas wish.

4

*E*milie refused to let Garrett help her retrieve a multitude of red storage tubs from what she described as a postage stamp–sized storeroom between the kitchen and the back door of the coffee shop, which she told Garrett opened to the alley running behind Main Street. She'd labeled the lid of each container, so it only took them a moment to find the lights. Emilie had labeled each colorful strand with the window it fit and stacked them in numerical order. A numbered diagram illustrated precisely where to place all twenty-seven strands.

Twenty-seven. Garrett imagined the entire coffee shop could fit inside a temporary supply shed on the base.

No more than twenty feet wide and maybe forty-five feet tall, Brew's two-story, brick shop front celebrated the magnificent attention to stability and detail so often seen in architecture from the late nineteenth century. A recessed, glass double-door entry provided shelter from the weather. Thin cast iron-framed large display windows with smaller transoms above them decorated either side of the entrance. At the height of a second level, double-hung, sash-and-frame windows allowed generous amounts of natural light into the upstairs, which Garrett assumed acted as office or living space, since Emilie had retrieved the holiday tubs from the lower level. A sucker for fantastic craftsmanship, Garrett would've enjoyed inspecting the building's decorative cornices and masonry corbeling. Hard to imagine the time and talent allotted to create such a structure.

Emilie buzzed into the kitchen, calling over her shoulder that she'd just be a second.

Garrett picked up the diagram — make that the *stapled packet* of diagrams — on top of the wound lights to study the drawings.

The top piece of paper, aged to the color of pale tea and sporting a faded yet distinct coffee cup ring over delicate cursive script, depicted swags of greenery and lights hung corner to corner in one of the two display windows. Ribbons and ornaments decorated the greenery, and a rocking chair sat beneath it. The drawing, detailed down to the gifts surrounding the wooden rocker and the quilt draped over it, made Garrett's fingers burn with the need to sketch. It was a twinge he hadn't felt in so long that he glanced down at his hands to be sure he hadn't imagined it.

"You good?" Emilie asked from behind Garrett, taking him by surprise. "Are your hands okay?"

Garrett glanced at them again to discover the twitch had progressed into a slight shake. He balled both fists and then spread his fingers wide, shaking off the sensation.

"Yeah, just stiff, I guess," he replied, as nonchalantly as he could muster. He hadn't drawn so much as a stick figure since joining the Marines, not counting routes sketched in dirt and easily erased. Why such powerful urges to study masonry and ironwork or hold a sketchpad in his hands now? "How can I help?"

Garrett didn't wait for Emilie's reply, stepping forward to take hold of the tall ladder she'd carried from the back.

"Miss Roanna liked to begin with *Window 1*, so that's what I do, too."

"These are her notes?"

"The most beautiful pages are," Emilie said, with a self-deprecating laugh in her voice. "The blob-ish drawings and much less elegant penmanship are mine," she added over her shoulder as Garrett followed her to the front corner of the shop. He helped Emilie move tables and chairs, set up the ladder, and tested strands of lights while she removed antiques and miscellaneous elements of fall decor that had been on display for Thanksgiving.

"You create the exact same window scenes every year?"

"It's a Brew tradition," she admitted with a grin. "Although I sneak in a few new elements each year."

"Sneak them in?"

"Without Mr. Moody knowing," she said in a stage whisper and with a rueful glance at the round table and the five remaining seniors, since Dr. Ramon had gone to take his family portraits and Ms. Cheyenne had left to meet up with her quilting group.

"I see." Garrett nodded knowingly. "What he doesn't know won't hurt him?"

"Yes!" Emilie said with flair. "That's a Brew tradition, too: not telling Mr. Moody what he doesn't *need to know*," she confessed with a laugh. "Roanna and I used to flip through magazine after magazine each fall, discovering the new holiday trends, finding fun crafting projects to host here at the shop, and secretly adding to the Christmas stash around here. I'm pretty sure Mr. Moody knew exactly what we were up to, but if he ever gave us a second glance, we feigned innocence and snuck our goodies and projects right under his nose."

"And Roanna was his wife?"

"Yes," Emilie answered with a heavy sigh. "The axis that balanced his world."

"I've noticed he's a bit…grouchy," Garrett pointed out, trying to be kind but also truthful. "Tough to envision him doting on anyone."

"His irritability is his armor. Since Roanna died, he's struggled. Beneath that gruff facade is a sweet old man with a shattered heart. His pain is simply more than he knows how to handle. Brew was Roanna's and Roanna was Brew; her stamp is on every single inch…the paintings, the fixtures, the furniture, the silverware pattern, the heavy coffee cups, and the vintage water goblets — she's everywhere. Now that she's gone, it hurts him too much to be here, but it hurts even more to stay away."

"When did she die?" Garrett asked.

"Almost four years ago. But the doctors diagnosed her with CJD less than a year before that, so it's been a really difficult five years for Mr. Moody." Sadness and reverence shadowed Emilie's voice.

"CJD?"

"Creutzfeldt–Jakob Disease," she said, her tone flipping from heavy to angry faster than a light switch. "It's similar to Alzheimer's disease but progresses very rapidly. There's not a single effective treatment out there for CJD, and certainly no cure. Like Alzheimer's disease, it's a death sentence, one that's devastating to witness in someone you love."

The fire extinguished in Emilie's eyes, replaced by a sheen of tears.

An open book, she wore everything she felt as plain as day on her beautiful face.

At first glance, Garrett would've described Emilie as cute,

like the *girl next door* or a buddy's little sister. Her long blonde hair hung in a perky ponytail. That and her petite stature gave him the impression she was quite a bit younger than his thirty-two years. But after watching her juggle patrons, serve food, refill beverages, take phone orders, and keep the dining room tidy and clean, he'd realized she was either incredibly mature for her age or more experienced than her youthful appearance led him to believe. Not that it mattered. Regardless of her actual age, she was decades younger than he felt, both physically and mentally. Perhaps spiritually, too. He'd avoided considering how long it had been since he'd had a conversation with God. Too long, Garrett didn't doubt, but sometimes opening the lines of communication felt like too daunting a hurdle. It was the same way he felt about his parents, a ten-hour drive from where he stood, but also ten years away from where he was at the moment.

"If you'll hold this while I climb, I'll hammer in the nails, and then you can feed the greenery and lights up to me a few feet at a time," Emilie said, extending an armful of artificial yet festive decorations.

She'd caught him lost in thought.

He looked at her armload, then back at her inquisitive cocoa eyes. The thick brows and dense eyelashes framing them brought to mind a fawn — one patient, wide-eyed, and curious, like in an animated Disney movie.

When Garrett still didn't catch up, she set down the heavy load draped across her arms and clasped her hands at her heart. Concern clouded those deer-like eyes. She bit her lip in hesitation.

His eyes grazed over her lips, supple and plump and promising.

"Garrett?" she asked in a soft voice, thankfully interrupting his thoughts once again. "Are you okay?"

How had he ever thought her merely *cute?*

How had he missed the empathy and kindness emanating from her every word and gesture?

Garrett acknowledged his heart thumping like a bass drum in his chest and pushed the awareness away — an awareness that Emilie awoke something inside him he'd believed to be dead, something akin to desire. Not just for a taste of her sweet, soft lips, although he was sorely tempted to try. And not just for an opportunity to wrap his arms around her slight yet strong body. Although he *did* wish he could tuck Emilie into his hollow frame. He'd like to wrap her in a hug, just so he could bask in her innate goodness. She was a siren's song that called to him like a beacon of light. Scariest of all, Emilie made him want to try.

With a forced nod, Garrett released the trance between them.

"How 'bout *I* do the climbing, and you direct me where to put the nails?" he asked, gently pulling the hammer from her hand and turning his attention to the ladder.

"Deal," she agreed with a heartfelt smile that had his attention turning right back to her. Before Garrett lost all focus again, Emilie bounded off to answer the shop phone.

Breathe, Banks. She's just a girl.

By the time she returned, he had decided to make that thought his new mantra and play it on a continuous loop in his fractured mind. Maybe that way he'd quit losing his mind over someone he'd barely met and truly didn't know.

5

Over the next several hours, Emilie corrected that last fact.

She talked about her immediate family — consisting of Mom and Dad, who were high school sweethearts, plus older brother, Jax, who owned an auto-mechanic garage in town. She described both sets of her grandparents. The four were lifelong friends who'd lived next door to one another for over fifty years and just one street over from their married children. Emilie regretted not having cousins, since both her parents were only children. But she admitted that knowing the same friends since the day she was born felt like having an entire tribe of cousins, so she was certain she hadn't missed out on too much. Next, and while Garrett dutifully followed Emilie's instructions to hang a nail there or move that greenery over another inch, she talked about attending Green Hills Elementary School, followed by Green Hills Junior High, and finally Green Hills High School, where she cheered for four years while also playing basketball, singing in the choir, and serving on the student government. After graduation, she spent a summer lifeguarding at the Green Hills Country Club before leaving home for college, where she joined a sorority, the French club, and helped launch a collegiate organization to partner with the Alzheimer's Association. Sadly, she explained, her volunteer work with dementia patients and their families proved incredibly helpful when Roanna received her diagnosis just months after Emilie had returned home, business degree in hand and eager to restart her life in her cherished hometown.

By the time they'd hung swags of greenery and lights in all the street-facing windows, secured the garland with thick strips of tartan fabric made into bows, and tucked picks of berries and boughs of holly along every inch of decor, Garrett knew Emilie's life history, the stories behind several prominent, founding families of the community, and the Green Hills origin story.

He had to admit that the time had flown by. Emilie's stories entertained him so much, he hadn't realized so much of the day had passed. She'd seemed content to do the talking, and Garrett was fine letting her carry the conversation. At times, he'd been tempted to share some of his own story. But in the end, he'd remained quiet through Emilie's pauses, letting her pick up the thread of narration as she felt like it. Garrett found her easy to listen to; she had a habit of framing a tale with just enough humor, often pointing the laugh at herself. She had a humble spirit and a good heart.

Thinking he wouldn't mind if their time together continued, Garrett contemplated asking her if she'd be willing to have dinner with him — since he didn't know anyone else in town and had no idea where to go for food. And technically, Brew had closed an hour earlier.

Climbing down the ladder after driving in the final nail and fastening the last bow, Garrett stepped to the floor just as Emilie stopped beside him. *Right* beside him. He froze midmotion.

She held the decorating instruction booklet up for them to look at together.

"Not a bad start," she said, glowing with joy as she compared the drawings to the holiday scene they'd created in the windows.

"A start?" Garrett echoed, somewhat choking on the words.

Why was she standing so close…with her shoulder and arm nearly touching his chest and ribs?

And, Dear Lord, why does she smell so good? Like cinnamon and cloves with a hint of roses. The fragrance filled his head with a hum. *Seriously, throw me a line. Please.*

It didn't escape Garrett's notice that he'd just asked God a legitimate question for the first time in— well, a long time. He hadn't hesitated, though, hadn't thought twice. Reopening that line of communication wasn't nearly as difficult as he'd made it out to be.

"I'll come in early to set up the tree and add a few more decorations," she explained, smiling up at him with a devious gleam in her eyes. "But I'd say we *nailed it.*"

Emilie covered her mouth to hold back a giggle, and her silly play on words eased Garrett's tense nerves. Later, he'd worry about why — and how — she got him tied in knots so quickly.

"So, we're done?" he asked, ecstatic to hear his voice sounding normal and not like a predator on the prowl.

"Almost. Since we've already got the ladder out, I want to hang some mistletoe outside the entrance." Without a second glance at Garrett, Emilie disappeared into the kitchen. She returned in less than a minute, wrapping florist wire around the ends of fresh-cut sprigs of what Garrett assumed was mistletoe; he'd never seen the stuff up close.

Emilie snagged a piece of twine from one of the storage tubs and gathered the shoots into a bouquet, tying the skinny rope around the stalks several times before knotting it tight. Then she fished through the container for another strip of plaid fabric, and repeated the process, wrapping it around the twine several times before tying a bow.

Without grabbing a coat, Emilie headed to the front doors. Garrett followed with the ladder.

"*Brrr!*" Emilie exclaimed when a blustery wind met them head-on. "The temperature's really dropped," she commented, hopping up and down to get warm as Garrett unfolded the ladder again.

Before he knew it, Emilie had climbed several rungs.

"I can hang that for you," Garrett offered.

"Aww, thank you." She smiled down at him before returning to her climb. "But it's kinda my thing. You know, like saving the angel for Dad to put on top of the tree every year? I've been hanging the mistletoe out here since I was a teenager."

Balanced on the top step, with her cheeks flushed and golden hair fluttering about, Emilie looked like an angel. An entrancing, exquisite, extraordinary—

In the blink of an eye, and at the exact moment hard truths about his attraction to her hit Garrett square in the gut, Emilie shifted, extending her arms high to reach the base of the light fixture under the eave and accidentally kicking the ladder out from under her feet.

With a soldier's speed and instinctual response, Garrett pushed the ladder away and caught Emilie in his arms. She landed against his chest with a thud, extracting a shocked squeal from Emilie and a grunt of pain from Garrett.

"Oh, Garrett, I'm so sorry," she hastened to apologize, but

Garrett needed a second to catch his breath. Maybe a few minutes. His eye twitched as he mentally instructed his back to relax. He couldn't set her down until it did; he couldn't move at all.

Deep inhales. Slower exhales. Visualize oxygen releasing the tension. Breathe past it.

Garrett closed his eyes, partly against the agony in his back and partly because he couldn't watch her watching him. Not in that moment.

Emilie wrapped her arms around his shoulders, lifting herself in a way that lightened the pressure on his spine. She'd told him all about flying as a cheerleader…that must've been where she learned such body control. "Just let my legs go," she whispered. "I'll ease to the ground."

He focused on doing just that, letting her legs slide from his hold. Her whole body slid down his until her toes connected with the tiled floor outside the coffee shop.

Emilie shivered, alerting Garrett to two facts: number one, she was freezing; and number two, she hadn't stepped from the shelter of his frame.

"Garrett," she said in a quiet voice. She was too intuitive, saw too much.

When he still couldn't meet her gaze, Emilie placed her palms against his cheeks, forcing his eyes to meet hers. Garrett searched her face for signs of pity, but he couldn't find any.

"Thank you."

He tried once more to look away from her sweet gratitude. Garrett didn't want it. He wanted to be whole, to be healthy. To carry a stunning woman in his arms without his injuries flaming to life, to be the hero someone like Emilie deserved.

She refused to let him avoid her. Instead, she tightened her hold, gripping his jaw with one hand and wrapping the other behind his neck. "Garrett," she said again, his name a praise on her lips. "You caught me. I could've been hurt — badly —

if I'd hit the ground, falling from the top of that twelve-foot ladder. *Thank you,*" she repeated. Then Emilie pulled his cheek down until, perched on her tippy-toes, she could place her lips against his warm skin for a fleeting moment.

Then, she studied his eyes for another split second, offered a somber smile that didn't reach her eyes, and bent to right the ladder before folding and carrying it inside.

Garrett watched her go. Like the proverbial deer in the headlights, he stood frozen in place. He'd never run from a challenge, but he'd never wanted to flee so much.

It wasn't Emilie; she was great. Incredible, really.

If he could go back in time…if he wasn't broken — *if, if, if.*

But Garrett couldn't, and he *was* damaged.

So, he took one rueful look at the mistletoe hanging overhead, touched the skin where she'd kissed his cheek, and walked away.

6

***The key to victory lies more in
manipulation and cooperation
than in exceptional personal skills.
Yuval Noah Harari***

Soldiers are known for their self-discipline.

Their stringent self-control is often the difference between life and death.

They have no problem with self-sacrifice if that's what is best for others.

So, why did I make it all of two days before I came back to my seat at her coffee shop? Garrett berated himself as he slid onto the stool.

His nerves jangled as he pretended to study the menu.

He couldn't stop his fingers from strumming on the counter or his foot from bouncing on the rail.

Both came to an abrupt halt when an older woman he'd never seen before approached with a cup of coffee.

"Cream or sugar?" she asked in place of a warm welcome.

"No," Garrett spat. "No, thank you, I mean," he amended when the rough tone of his voice caused those within earshot to frown his way. "Just black, please. And thank you," he added, stumbling over his words. He started to ask, *Why are you here? And where is the lovely angel I came to see?* But Garrett thought better of it just in the nick of time and swallowed his words with a gulp of his coffee.

Not as good as Emilie's.

He slow-sipped three mugs of sludge, but she still hadn't appeared, and he couldn't stand another cup.

Garrett tossed a ten-dollar bill on the bar, gathered his jacket, and accepted defeat.

"You helped hang all this hoopla?" a gruff voice asked from across the dining room as Garrett walked toward the front doors.

Everyone in the shop stopped what they were doing, but no one else answered, so Garrett assumed Mr. Moody had spoken to *him*.

"If you mean the twenty-seven strands of lights, hundreds of feet of greenery, and box after box of holiday decor that Emilie turned into a winter wonderland to attract your customers, then yes, I helped with the hoopla."

Mr. Moody eyed Garrett, dislike clearly evident in the man's pursed frown.

The woman sitting beside Mr. Moody — a striking Native American with flawless skin and jet-black hair — responded with delight.

"Mr. Banks," she said with quiet authority. "Please come sit with us before you leave."

Mr. Moody grunted but didn't rebuke or rescind her invitation.

"Yes," another woman said in a lilting voice. "Please join us, Mr. Banks."

"Garrett," he corrected. "Just Garrett is fine."

"Garrett," the robust man who'd been wearing the gaudy Christmas sweater a few days earlier said with hearty and genuine-sounding pleasure. "It's nice to meet you. I'm Dr. Ramon— Well, I used to be," he corrected. "But my doctoring days are over, though everyone still calls me Doc, or Alden, which is my actual name." The elderly man reached forward to shake Garrett's hand as Garrett walked past him to reach the only empty chair at their large, round table. "So, you're staying at the Conrad."

He'd stated it, not asked.

"It's—" A third woman started to speak, but a boisterous sneeze from the man next to her interrupted. She shook her head, eyeing him with a look of indifference while the fellow pulled out a handkerchief and put it to good use. When he'd finished and stowed away his rag, she turned heavy-lidded eyes back to Garrett. "As I was about to say, it's such a lovely hotel…but not inexpensive. How long will you be there?"

She didn't mince words. Nope, the innocuous smiles plastered on all but one face at the table didn't fool Garrett. *This crew is out for information.*

What had Emilie called them…her super seniors? She'd detailed each one's unique gifts and quirky traits when she'd described all her favorite people in Green Hills while they'd decorated for Christmas.

Garrett had known Mr. Moody right off, without hearing Emilie's description. She swore he had a huge heart under all that petulance, but Garrett had yet to see proof.

He didn't recall the rest of their names, but he could identify each from what she'd told him about their lives and their legacies…the brilliant doctor, the bashful beauty, the sneezy schoolteacher, the writing night owl, the happy artist, and the silent soldier.

What might appear to be a ragtag group of retirees meant the world to Emilie. Therefore, Garrett sought to make a good impression. And he really wanted to find Emilie.

First order of business? Make up for his snippy response to Mr. Moody's question.

As any good interrogator knows, one must give in order to receive. Knowledge is power, especially to a group of older folks who spend much of their time with one another, sitting around the same table at the same coffee shop, day after day. Thus, sharing information builds trust and is often the quickest way to get what one wants: intel of their own.

As in, where's Emilie?

"Yes, ma'am. You're right about the hotel," Garrett said, addressing the author. "It's fancier than I need, but it was the first thing I saw when I drove into town a few days ago. Luckily, they offer a military discount, which makes the rate more reasonable."

"You could always rent a room — if you'll be staying a while," the artist offered.

"At the lake? The other day Emilie mentioned a lodge with cabins. Just a few minutes from town?" he asked, happy to relinquish the floor.

Garrett's ploy worked; the super seniors gave him directions to Daisy Lake and the lodge, they listed which individuals owned and offered short-term rentals, and they lamented that the Primrose Cottages still sat empty on the outskirts of town.

Garrett noticed the abandoned roadside cabins on his way to Green Hills. Slowing as he drove by, his architect's soul had imagined the property in its heyday…individual tiny houses — before tiny houses were a trend — each with its own driveway and carport, forming a U-shape around a gathering place in the center, which included a swimming pool, picnic tables and grills, and a small playground for the kids.

But he wasn't an architect; Garrett was a soldier. An accomplished one at that. And the Primrose Cottages looked to be dilapidated and crumbling and nothing like a 1940s tourist attraction. They had that in common: both once-great, they'd become redundant, obsolete, hollowed-out, and as far from their intended purpose as could be.

The mention of Emilie's name pulled Garrett out of his pity party.

He schooled his features into nonchalance before lifting his gaze to reenter the conversation. His eyes locked with the one senior who'd yet to speak. Emilie'd said he wouldn't, that the veteran hadn't uttered a word since returning home from the war. Garrett respected that. If it wasn't specific to his life as a Marine, he had little to talk about either. He gave the gentleman a deferential nod, and the man's face lit up with an animated smile.

"…surely Jinx will send someone to help her," the first woman said under her breath, more of a hope than a statement.

"Surely," the artist agreed. "Jinx takes such good care of her…always so eager to lend her a hand."

"She's fine," Mr. Moody retorted. "Perfectly capable of fixing stuff around here. Does it all the time."

"Emilie has no business reframing and replacing that old door in the back," the writer scoffed, which got Garrett's full attention.

"Jinx?" he asked, stuck on the guy who was of such great value to Emilie.

"Malone," Doc answered. "Owns Malone's Hardware out on the highway. Emilie's gone there to get supplies for a… project she's determined to do. Probably back by now, though." He'd hesitated and made a face at Mr. Moody on the word *project*, as if he'd wanted to say something else.

"She's your manager, Alfy, not a handyman," the school-teacher commented from behind the open newspaper in his hands. Garrett couldn't be sure if he was reading it or simply using it to shield the group from his allergies.

"She's the one set on fixing the place up, determined to

change things that've worked just fine for years. I'm just letting her do what she wants," Mr. Moody said, hands up in innocent justification.

"Emilie wants to buy equipment that'll bring this place into the twenty-first century, not become a construction worker. Enough with the Band-Aids and duct tape — they're about as effective as rearranging deck chairs on the Titanic," the writer argued.

"I don't know, Alora. I think this place needs both. A fresh coat of paint and one of those newfangled barista machines would go a long way toward keeping her here," the pretty woman with the wild curls of white hair offered with a hopeful twinkle in her eyes.

So Doc was the doctor, Mr. Moody was Alfy, and the writer was Alora. Three down, four to go.

"I'm not buying…*anything*," Mr. Moody growled. "But she's free to touch up paint all she wants," he allowed, as though granting her greatest wish.

"Do *not* put that on her plate." Alora pointed a butter knife at the old man, emphasizing each word with intimidation. "You've already got her trying to keep freezers afloat, repairing the back door, and reinforcing shelves in the storeroom. And that's on top of her actual job running the coffee shop, which is enough to keep *two* people busy 'round the clock."

"Don't forget the Christmas Eve festival," the artist with the awesome hair added, grinning from ear to ear.

"Blythe's right," Doc pointed out. "Prepping for the festival and getting ready for an influx of visitors that weekend is already asking too much of Emilie. We've got to find her some help."

Blythe — add another name to Garrett's growing list — shrugged her shoulders, but her face still glowed with merry anticipation for the festival.

The two quiet participants, the soldier and the beautiful

Native American woman, gazed into their coffee cups with forlorn expressions.

The teacher folded his newspaper, setting it aside in contemplation.

Mr. Moody *harrumphed*.

And Alora shook her knife at him with a menacing glare.

"I could help," Garrett heard himself say, shocking himself more than he surprised the rest of the group. "At least with the door and the storeroom shelves. I've got some construction experience," he added by way of a resume, as if they'd turn him down if he wasn't qualified.

Alora's assessing gaze made him want to squirm in his seat.

The teacher's satisfied nod boosted his confidence.

Blythe's face became even more enchanted, and the two silent souls beamed with pride, further convincing Garrett he'd done something wonderful.

"Are you sure, son?" Doc asked. "It's several days' worth of work," he offered as an out.

"Yeah, I'm sure."

Mr. Moody *harrumphed* again.

7

———

God lends a helping hand
to the man who tries hard.
Aeschylus

"We should check for gaps between the door and the frame before you attach those new hinges."

Emilie jumped sky-high, both startled and soothed by Garrett's deep voice behind her.

He'd vanished into the night after saving her life — or at least a limb. She hadn't seen him in the days since.

With a hand pressed against her galloping heart, she turned to face him.

"Hi." Two letters. *Impressive, Em.*

But she couldn't come up with anything more. Drinking in the sight of him robbed her of speech.

Dark-green camouflage did little to conceal his long, muscled legs. He'd tucked the hem of the pants into black work boots. The neckline of a white undershirt peeked from beneath a long-sleeved henley. The thick thermal knit accentuated his shoulders, biceps, and pecs before hanging loose over his stomach. Her traitorous brain conjured an image of washboard abs.

Stupid imagination.

But Emilie's self-recrimination did little good.

Her fingers itched to test the contrast of the soft shirt against a taut body, to trace the outline of his dog tags hanging against his chest.

Say something. Just…do something.

In response to her internal commands, Emilie clasped both hands behind her back. Still no words.

"I understand you're replacing a door," Garrett said, apparently unaffected by Emilie's inability to function in his presence. "Can I take a look?"

He moved toward the open doorframe without waiting for Emilie to respond. He casually ran a hand down her upper arm as he brushed past her. The friendly gesture — though completely platonic — left a sweep of flesh begging for his touch and sent tingles to her toes.

Oh, Lord…help me snap out of it!

"Did you happen to buy a new threshold, too?" Garrett asked, squatting down to run a hand over the rotted one.

Don't look. Don't look. Don't look.

"*Hmm?*" she strangled out of her throat.

"In fact, if you have enough lumber, it'd be best if we replaced the entire frame. This one's in pretty bad shape."

Garrett stood and faced Emilie.

"Why are you here?" she asked, her mind *finally* tracking.

"I came to see— I came for coffee. On my way out, your seniors summoned me to their table. They mentioned you were doing some carpentry, which happens to be one of my specialties…so, here I am," he said with a modest shrug.

"They shouldn't have asked you to do that. Really, I can figure it out."

"They didn't ask. I offered."

"You offered? How did my project even come up in conversation?"

Garrett thought for a second. "I honestly don't know. Someone said something about the hardware store owner sending help; then someone else said you shouldn't be Moody's handyman. Alora said something about deck chairs on the Titanic, and then Moody said you could paint all you like."

"He did?" Emilie gawked.

"Maybe. The rest of them agreed that you already have too much to do. Then Blythe got giddy over a festival, and I offered to hang the door."

"Oh, Garrett," Emilie said. An apologetic and angelic smile touched her face. "You've been played."

"I've been…?"

"Bamboozled, tricked, hoodwinked, conned, duped, deceived…*played*," Emilie repeated.

"*Huh.*" Garrett seemed almost impressed.

"I'm sorry. They shouldn't have roped you into volunteering for service," Emilie gushed. "Ms. Cheyenne complimented me on the decorations when they arrived the morning after we hung everything. I explained I hadn't done it alone and how you'd been an incredible help. That must've gotten their wheels turning. They might seem harmless, but they're anything but. You've been set up. In fact, I imagine *we've* been set up."

With another expression of thoughtful consideration, Garrett let the information simmer for a moment before looking over the tools and materials strewn about on either side of the missing door.

"Well, I'm already here, and you've got to be freezing," he said. "It looks like you have everything except the new threshold and weatherstrip. If you'll run back to the hardware store, I'll get started here."

"They'll think they've won," Emilie countered.

"Let 'em," he said, lifting one shoulder in serene acceptance. Then he offered Emilie the closest thing to a convincing smile she'd seen on his handsome face so far.

"Will it— I mean, I don't want to—"

Garrett gave Emilie his full attention.

"What about your back?" she asked as tenderly as she could. The stark pain she'd seen him in a few days earlier still haunted her. She'd feel awful if she caused it again.

A veil fell over Garrett's eyes. His jaw ticked.

"It's fine," he said in a clipped tone.

"I'm sorry, Garrett. I didn't mean to upset you. I just don't want to—"

"You won't," he said, cutting her off. "Run and get that threshold. I'll be ready for it by the time you get back."

The entire drive to Jinx's store and all the way back, Emilie's mind spun like a hamster on a wheel.

She enjoyed spending time with Garrett and would like to find more time to get to know him.

But he wasn't very forthcoming with personal details…like, *at all.* She had no idea how long he planned to be in Green Hills, where he'd been stationed last, or if/when he'd return. Where was his life? What about his family? What did he call home? Something had happened; he was definitely injured. But was that new or old, temporary or chronic? What was he doing there, and for that matter, *who* was he? He'd shared nothing.

She was simply drawn to him.

Which was silly. And potentially unwise, since she might not be in Green Hills much longer herself.

Emilie had thought Mr. Moody would resurface from his grief after losing Roanna. She'd expected it to take a while, but almost four years later, her boss was only getting more and more difficult to work for.

Emilie had offered to buy Brew several times. She'd worked

with Blake Fisher, a local real estate agent, to write a fair and rewarding contract. Emilie had gone so far as to obtain financing from the local bank.

Mr. Moody had refused to even look at the paperwork.

He didn't want to deal with the business, but he wouldn't consider letting it go, either…a lose-lose situation for all.

It wasn't just about updating the interior, the menu, and the equipment, although Green Hills deserved a modern coffeehouse experience. She'd never stray far from Roanna's vision for Brew, never disturb the history and reverence of the antique building. But Emilie had worked hard to earn her degree, hone her business acumen, and develop experience. She'd saved relentlessly, and she had dreams and goals and hopes for her future.

She wanted to roast.

In college, Emilie enrolled in an elective course about coffee profiles. By the end of the first class, she'd been hooked. The next semester, she'd begun working on a minor in roasting science. The following summer, she'd interned with a mill in Minneapolis, where she'd been a member of their in-house roastery team. She'd learned about bean profiles, discovered private label production, and fallen in love with custom blending techniques.

In her evenings, she'd spent the past few years taking online classes, becoming a Certified Coffee Specialist, and working toward the Master of Coffee credential. If she could just eliminate some of the day-to-day fires that needed her attention at Brew, she could add a small-batch roastery to bolster their bottom line and bring new attention to Green Hills.

In her dreams, Emilie saw the whole endeavor in brilliant detail…the roasting logo, their preprinted to-go cups, and a swanky website for promotion. When she closed her eyes, she could almost smell the custom blends she'd create.

Hadn't she put those visions on hold for long enough?

If Mr. Moody wouldn't — or couldn't — allow Emilie to move forward, she'd have no choice but to move away.

In the words of Scarlett O'Hara, I'll think about that tomorrow.

Parking in the alley behind Brew, Emilie recited the famous line from *Gone with the Wind* for the hundredth time that month, and the month was still young.

She grabbed the hardware supplies from the passenger seat and huddled into her coat to ignore the arctic bite in the air.

"Perfect timing," Garrett announced as he checked a builder's level against a board he'd installed to construct a new frame. "And…perfectly level," he announced. His voice sounded relaxed, even pleased. It sounded good.

"Yes, well, Jinx said this should work." Emilie handed over the metal piece and a roll of rubber weather stripping. "What's all this?" she asked, gesturing toward a pile of small wood pieces that hadn't been there when she left.

"Shims," Garrett answered. "We'll use them to square-up the door and fill in gaps before putting trim around the frame."

"Where did they come from?"

"I shaved them off the old door. Figured you could spare a few inches off the bottom."

"I was going to throw it away."

"What?" he teased. "It's a great door. You can't just toss it in the trash."

Not just relaxed, he was downright *playful*. It seemed a job Emilie had dreaded and postponed until the door was literally hanging by a single screw positively made Garrett's day.

"But what will I do with it?" she asked, happy to play along.

"Do you trust me?" Garrett asked. His tone, albeit still jovial, held a hint of need, like her answer mattered.

Their eyes snapped to one another's. Emilie's heart skipped a beat. She studied his earnest expression while he waited patiently for her response.

"Yes, Garrett. I believe I do."

8

———

You can make bad choices
and find yourself in a downward spiral
or you can find something
that gets you out of it.
Ray LaMontagne

Garrett smiled.

Not a half-smile, not a quiet chuckle, and not a forced nicety.

His face — already chiseled and tanned and the type fantasies were made of — transformed.

If austere, intense, controlled Garrett made Emilie's pulse quicken, then chipper, vivacious, effervescent Garrett might do her in completely.

But what a way to go!

"You're freezing again," he said. "Go on…get inside."

"And you aren't even wearing a jacket," Emilie argued.

"I'm good," he promised, and Emilie believed him.

Two hours later, she went looking for Garrett, wanting to

check on him, but also with an offer to fix him something warm for lunch.

She found him in the larger storeroom they used as a pantry and receiving area, with a pencil behind his ear and a tape measure in his hand. He'd stacked the cans and boxes and bags of food items on one set of rickety metal shelves and pushed the paper goods to one corner.

"You worked right through the lunch rush," Emilie said, announcing her presence. He looked so lost in thought, she hadn't wanted to startle him. She walked over to see what he'd written on a torn sheet of butcher paper. "Garrett, this is incredible," she exclaimed, astounded by the renderings he'd drawn of a remodeled, high-functioning, *fabulous* storage area. Emilie picked up the sketch to study it closer. "Are these floor-to-ceiling shelves built in? With a rolling ladder on a track? And a separate closet for the cleaning supplies, instead of propped in the hallway? That would be so nice! And what's this?" She pointed to the fourth wall, the one that backed up to the hallway.

"Just a place for equipment," he said, like it was nothing.

"I saw them stacked in every nook and cranny of the kitchen when I walked through and thought it would be nice to keep them organized and easier to reach."

"Hooks to hang the pots and pans? Lower shelves for heavier trays and special event pieces? Plenty of room for larger skillets and woks? Garrett, I don't know what to say… this is unbelievable. Truly, if you show this one area to Byron, beware…he'll probably try to kiss you!"

Garrett waved off her compliments, but Emilie wouldn't have it as she continued raving over the detail and perfection of his design.

"If I ever convince Mr. Moody to spend a little money on upgrades," she told him, "this is exactly what I'll have built."

"*I'm* building it," Garrett protested.

"What?" Emilie dropped the hand holding the blueprint to her side and whipped her head around to gaze up at Garrett. Had he been standing that close all along?

"*Reinforce storeroom shelves,*" he said, inching even closer. "It was on the list the seniors gave me this morning."

"Garrett." Emilie whispered his name on a faint breath.

He smiled down at her awestruck face and lifted a hand to smooth away a strand of hair stuck to her lip gloss. His eyes never left hers.

"Now *I* want to kiss you," she said in a barely audible voice.

"I wouldn't say no to that," Garrett replied, a half-smile tugging at his lips.

Heat flooded Emilie's cheeks.

Garrett chuckled, running his knuckles down her flaming skin.

"But I think you mentioned lunch, and since my favorite waitress at the coffee shop was MIA this morning, I haven't eaten all day." He stepped back, allowing Emilie to inflate her lungs, which helped since she'd been on the verge of fainting at his enthralling touch.

"Yes. Yes," she said again, gathering her wits and coming back to earth. "Stew. We have stew. To eat. For lunch. It's really good. And hot." So, maybe she hadn't gathered her wits as effectively as she'd hoped.

"That sounds good," Garrett said, kind enough to suppress another laugh — but rakish enough to wink at her as he pulled the drawing from her hand. "After you," he told her, waiting to follow her to the dining room.

There he sat at his usual countertop seat and fidgeted with the sketch while Emilie got him an enormous bowl of the soup, a bread plate piled with cornbread, a side salad, and a glass of ice water.

"Anything else? Maybe something else to drink?" she asked, setting everything in front of him. "Coffee? Iced tea? Soda?"

"Salt and pepper?" Garrett asked.

"Don't let Byron hear you," she said, like it was a dramatic secret as she slid a set of shakers from further down the bar.

"And you."

"And me…what?"

"Will you join me? To eat?"

"Oh, well…" Her voice tapered off. She glanced around the dining room to see the seniors deep in a conversation while finishing their dessert of cranberry-apple crumble, a woman sipping coffee and reading a book by the front window, and a couple holding hands and chatting after their meal.

"No one seems to need you right now," Garrett pointed out. "Except me."

"Okay," Emilie agreed. "I'll just grab a bowl."

When she returned with a smaller portion of stew and a glass of water, Garrett had moved down one stool. Emilie slid onto the one he'd vacated and appreciated that he'd warmed the chilly vinyl for her.

"Here," he said, holding out a buttered square of cornbread. "That's like a slice of heaven."

"Thank you," she replied, happily accepting the cornbread. She'd given him all they had left, and it was one of her favorites. "The recipe's a family secret."

"You made it? Byron lets you in his kitchen?"

"Didn't take long for you to figure him out," she laughed. "But yes, I'm allowed in *before* he arrives. I bake some of the bread, cakes, pies, and pastries to help out. We're a small army, so I don't mind double duty."

"Let me assure you, even in a big army, everyone pulls extra shifts."

"I'm sure that's true. Sometimes I wonder if we like to

make things a little harder than they have to be around here. Would the road be less bumpy if I followed a different path?"

"I think you've got a pretty good thing here. I'd say this place runs like a well-oiled machine. Your family's close; you're surrounded by friends and fond memories. There are a lot worse ways to live."

"Without a doubt," Emilie agreed. "I love it here. Green Hills is the only place I've ever wanted to be. I missed it so much during college. One summer, I worked at an internship instead of coming home…it almost broke me." She shuffled her feet, looking down and shaking her head at the recollection. "That sounds pretty pathetic, I imagine. Especially to you."

"To me?" Garrett asked.

"I'm guessing you've traveled the world, seen people and places I can't even imagine."

"That's true," he allowed. Garrett started to say more, but a shadow darkened his eyes. Then he shifted his attention back to his food and took a few bites. "You have nothing to be ashamed of, Emilie. Home is always the best place on earth."

"Thanks," she said with a grateful smile.

"And I can tell you that right now, Green Hills is the only place I want to be, too," Garrett said. His expression said there was more to that, but Emilie might've imagined what she wanted to see.

Emilie waited, hoping he'd tell her where home was for him. Did he have family expecting him for Christmas?

But he didn't offer, and she didn't ask.

When she finished eating, Emilie slid her dishes to the side, wiped the counter with her napkin, and pulled the store-room drawing close to study it again. Garrett continued eating, but he kept an obvious eye on Emilie at the same time.

The sketch was a piece of art. Even without a ruler, he'd

gotten the perspective just right. Everything appeared perfectly scaled. It looked like a professional rendering.

"Garrett, what do you do in the Marines?"

"Why do you ask?"

Emilie paused at the way he answered her question with a question. She didn't want to pry, but she did want to know… more. More about Garrett, where he came from, where he was going. What he liked…what he loved. His presence brought her peace, maybe because the time they'd spent together had been all about lightening her load and making her life easier. But it felt deeper than that, like she could happily sit in his company — quiet or chatty, working or resting, day or night — indefinitely. It was an odd feeling, but a nice one.

"This could be the work of a professional designer," she finally said.

Garrett stared at his bowl for a moment. Then he nodded his head and met her gaze. He exhaled a sigh, and then he shared…

"My dad's an architect. From the time I was old enough to walk, I lived under his feet. If he was drafting at home, I was right next to his chair, coloring or scribbling or drawing. If he had design meetings with clients, I begged to tag along. All I ever wanted to be was *him*. In elementary school, he started teaching me the fundamentals of drawing. During middle school, he explained historical elements and theories of modern design, and I kept sketching. In high school, I studied structural engineering. By then, I'd become a decent designer and could hold my own with my drafting skills.

"But my friends weren't as certain about what they wanted to do when they grew up. They started partying, even experimenting with drugs. A few of them got into some bad stuff. It's tough for a teenage boy to abandon his guys, even when he knows better. I made stupid choices, and they cost me everything. When a judge offered the military, I saw it as a way out, and more importantly, a way to escape the disappointment and disgust in my dad's eyes. The rest is history."

He pushed his empty dishes aside and looked directly into Emilie's face, looking — hoping? — for a reaction. She didn't give him one. Instead, she matched his scrutiny ounce for ounce. When he reached for his water, Emilie regarded the drawing in front of her again.

"You're talented."

He didn't reply.

"Do you miss it?" she asked, trying again.

"It's impossible to miss something you never had," he answered.

"Is it?"

His eyes darted over her features, but he said nothing.

Emilie gathered their plates and bowls and carried them into the kitchen rather than leaving them in the bin of soapy water on the rolling bussing cart. She returned with a large bowl of dessert covered in vanilla ice cream and two spoons.

"We're sharing," she announced, climbing back onto her stool and setting the bowl between them.

She handed a spoon to Garrett and waited for him to take the first bite.

"Did you make this, too?" he asked.

"Do you like it?" she asked, tilting her chin and resorting to his tit-for-tat style of communication.

"Yeah, it's delicious," he admitted, smiling at her attempt to be sassy.

"In that case, I did," she admitted, relaxing into her normal demeanor and dipping into the bowl for a bite. "And I'm glad you do."

"Do you cook, too, or just bake mouthwatering sweets?"

"We haven't even finished *this* late lunch," Emilie pointed out. "Are you already fishing for a dinner invitation?" Her sauciness returned in full force.

Garrett's smile turned into a sly, knowing grin.

"I wouldn't say no to that either."

Emilie's face flushed, just as it had when he'd said those exact words about kissing her.

I've lost my mind. Flirting — shamelessly — with someone so obviously out of my league.

Feigning innocence, Garrett returned to the cranberry-apple crumble.

"Well, you're out of luck," Emilie finally said, anything but sorry. "Because I'm not making dinner tonight."

"Guess I'd better buy a bowl of stew to go."

"But I *am* cooking tomorrow," she said in a genuine tone. "It's Sunday, so the shop is closed all day. I usually make supper around five o'clock, if you'd like to join me."

Stop apologizing for your gifts.
Ashli Montgomery

Garrett had accepted Emilie's invitation.

She hadn't mentioned his attending church with her. A twinge of guilt assaulted her for not asking, but he hadn't mentioned it, either. And honestly, she had been so shocked that he'd opened up about his childhood that she hadn't thought it wise to push her luck.

In the end, Garrett had asked if she would unlock the shop for him early that morning. He wanted to get started on the storeroom and hoped to take advantage of its being empty for the day.

Emilie had gotten up early, dressed for church, and gone to Brew around 7:00 a.m. She had barely put the coffee on when he arrived. He got right to work, taking one short break when she presented him with a plate filled with scrambled eggs, bacon, and a fat cinnamon roll, and stopping for another brief pause when she'd left for church.

After services, she ran by the grocery store, stocking up for the week. When she got home, she changed into comfy clothes, put away her groceries, prepped a casserole for their dinner, and curled up on the couch with a sweet holiday romance novel.

At 4:30, a timer sounded on her phone, alerting Emilie that she needed to slide the casserole into the oven to heat.

She indulged in one — maybe two — more chapters before closing her book to put a vintage Christmas album on her turntable, set the dining room table, and toss a salad.

The doorbell chimed at exactly 4:50.

"You're early," Emilie said as she opened the front door.

"Five minutes early is five minutes late," he replied, holding out his fists. "Pick one," he told her.

"Like, pick a card, any card?" she asked, surprised by his boyish antics.

"Exactly."

"Okay, I choose this one." She placed her hand over his, turning it until his palm opened up, revealing her key to Brew. She'd left it with him to lock up when he finished working.

"There's your key to Brew," he announced, leaving her at the open door when he stepped past her.

"Wait," she called, turning to catch up, "what was in the other hand?"

"Guess we'll never know," he hedged, all innocent and playful. "I created a bit of sawdust in the shop today, and I don't want to track it inside your house. Mind if I take off my boots?"

"Not at all. Make yourself comfortable."

He did just that, draping his jacket over a wingback chair by the front door and leaving his boots beside it.

Next, Garrett surveyed her home, taking in the decor and knickknacks while wearing a goofy expression.

Emilie wondered if he realized how his spirits lifted when he worked with his hands. She recognized it when he took over the door replacement. She had seen it in his eyes when she'd discovered him planning the storeroom remodel. And he'd just proven it, arriving in such a good mood after a day of demolition. Emilie could only imagine how happy he'd be when actual construction began.

The thought brought with it a twinge of worry.

She hadn't forgotten the pain in his back when she fell off the ladder, but she didn't intend to spoil his delight by asking about it again.

The concern must've weighed on her heart or festered in the back of her mind because the topic arose of its own accord during dinner.

She had brought the casserole dish to the table, along with the salad and homemade challah bread, which she'd sliced, buttered, and toasted in the oven. Since she usually ate alone, Emilie rarely used her formal dining table. When they sat down to eat, she pointed him toward the head of the table without conscious thought. She took the seat to his right, nearer to the serving pieces in the center of the table.

She filled both plates while Garrett poured their glasses of iced tea from the glass pitcher she'd set on the table, and then they enjoyed dinner.

Garrett complimented her cooking. Emilie again basked in his praise.

She asked what he'd done with the storeroom, and he detailed how he'd removed the old shelves, cleaned the space top to bottom, and marked measurements for the carpentry work.

He finished his first helping of baked spaghetti at the same time he finished explaining the materials and supplies he hoped to find at Malone's Hardware on Monday morning.

"Ready for more?" Emilie asked, reaching for Garrett's plate. She'd already come to realize he had an enormous appetite and liked to eat. She had also accepted that feeding others must be one of her love languages; she relished the way he devoured her cooking.

"I've got it," he said when she moved to stand up. But when he leaned at an angle to pick up the dish, he must've twisted his spine in an unfortunate way, because he grunted in distress and plopped back into his chair, a sheen of sweat already popping on his brow.

"Garrett—"

Her arms flew toward him, but his expression of excruciating pain stopped her concerned cry.

It was as if he couldn't even breathe.

He remained frozen in place, head down, eyes shut tight, and jaw tensed.

"What can I do?" Emilie whispered, desperate to help.

Garrett shook his head the tiniest bit but couldn't muster any more.

Emilie covered his hands, balled into fists on the table, with her own.

When he didn't rebuke her touch, she stood, coming around the end of the table to stand beside him.

With more caution than she would have approach a frightened animal, she moved a hand to his shoulder and gently squeezed. And again, until the repetition turned into a massage.

He relaxed a fraction of an inch, and his chin fell even closer to his chest.

Emilie moved her other hand to the back of his neck, kneading the tight cords.

"I'm so sorry," she whispered, needing to soothe and unsure what words might help.

Garrett's breath eventually evened. In time, he shifted to rest his forearms on the table. He held his head in his hands. Emilie continued to work the knots from his shoulders and neck, too afraid to do more harm to his back but also unable to sit by doing nothing.

After ten minutes — maybe even more — Garrett lifted his head and leaned back in his chair. His hands covered Emilie's on his shoulders. Then he drew one toward his lips, whispering an anguished, "Thank you," as he brushed a kiss across her palm.

Entwining their fingers, she refused to release his hand as she slid back into her chair, scooting it closer to his in one fluid motion.

"I'm so sorry," she repeated, sure he hadn't heard her before.

"It's not your fault." Garrett said, his words tight and guttural. Judging from his haunted gray pallor, pain continued to torment him.

"But if I hadn't let you hang all those decorations, and fix that door yesterday, and work on the storeroom for hours and hours today… You did all that for me."

"Who said I did that for you?" His attempt at humor didn't reach his eyes, nor his intended audience.

Emilie wiped a tear from her cheek that had fallen without permission.

"Please don't cry," Garrett begged. "Not for me, not for something you had nothing to do with."

She didn't believe him. That must've shown clearly on her face.

"Honestly, it comes and goes. I can go hours without it hurting, and then other times it's unrelenting."

"Hours? It hurts like that every day?" Emilie couldn't fathom such chronic misery.

"Nothing I've done these past few days has made any difference," he said, not answering her questions about how often he felt like that. "If anything, spending time with you has eased my pain."

"You can spend time with me *without* doing manual labor."

"Really? Why didn't you say so sooner?" he joked half-heartedly.

"Is it just your back?" Emilie asked, not willing to be side-tracked by his attempts to make *her* feel better, not when he looked so green around the gills. "Are you hurt in other ways, too?"

Garrett looked from their clasped hands to Emilie's face. He studied her, and while she didn't know what he was looking for, she hoped he saw that she genuinely cared. And that he could trust her, too.

He shifted, taking an intentional breath and slowly lengthening his spine to sit taller in his chair — a hard, wooden dining room chair that couldn't be all that comfortable.

"Let's go sit in the living room," she blurted out.

"Yeah, I don't think I can eat anymore. At least not right now," Garrett agreed, casting a wistful glance at his dinner plate.

"We'll reheat it later, if you want some."

"Thanks." His sad half-smile made Emilie feel worse. The way he winced when he stood made her downright sick.

"Can I do anything?" she asked, not sure whether to try to help or just stay out of his way.

"You're doing it," he answered, releasing her hand to swipe another errant tear from her cheek.

"And what is that?" She couldn't believe she had done anything besides cause him grief.

"You don't judge me when the pain hits," he said, taking long but slow strides toward the couch. "There's sympathy in your eyes but not pity. That's a bigger gift than you know." He released a stiff exhale as he lowered himself to sit at the end of the couch.

Emilie rushed to clear space on the coffee table for his feet and hand him every decorative throw pillow in the room, which made him smile — well, almost smile. Then she cleared the dining room table, covered the food with plastic wrap, and stuffed the leftovers in the fridge. It took less than five minutes to rinse their plates and silverware and load the dishwasher. Then she refilled their glasses and joined him on the couch, a bottle of over-the-counter pain medicine in her hand.

"Thanks," he said, taking the bottle and swallowing three pills with a drink of tea.

"I hope they help," she said, facing him and folding her legs crisscross on the cushion beside him.

The soft smile he cast her looked less strained, and the vise grip loosened on her heart.

But then Garrett leaned his head against the back of the couch, closing his eyes as if fighting another internal battle, and her stomach sank.

"Are you okay?" she asked. Worry filled every word.

Garrett opened his eyes, lifted his head, and extended a hand, palm up, toward her.

She grasped it without hesitation, holding it in her lap.

"I don't have PTSD," Garrett said, his tone flat and scientific. "Just the opposite, really. I *need* to go back. It's what I'm good at...*really* good at." He let that sink in, but Garrett didn't peel his eyes from their clasped hands, refusing to see her reaction. "I explained a little about your friend Noble, about our training."

"With the marsocks, right?"

"Close," he said with tender fondness. "MARSOC stands for Marine Corps Forces Special Operations Command. That's what I do, too. We're Marine Raiders...similar to Navy SEALs and Army Green Berets; we're special operators performing specialized missions."

"That sounds serious," Emilie said, suddenly overwhelmed with fear and dread. She tightened her grip on his hand.

"All military service is serious, but yes, our units are elite forces." Garrett stopped to get another drink of his tea with his other hand. Good, because Emilie had no intention of relinquishing the one she held. "You asked if I'd seen the world." Emilie nodded, even though Garrett still hadn't even glanced at her. "I have, but not the beautiful parts. We go to the worst parts, fight the worst people, and do whatever needs to be done to defeat them. That's our job."

Garrett finally lifted his gaze to look deep into Emilie's eyes. It was a test; she knew it was…a test to see if he'd shocked or offended her. But she met his challenge, refusing to look away. "That's what I do," he continued. "Maybe I should feel bad about it — what I've done. But I don't. I do what must be done, and like I said, I'm really good at it."

10

You can't heal what you don't acknowledge.
Jack Canfield

"*I* was really good at it," Garrett corrected.

"Was?" Emilie said. Her strength had impressed him; her determination to hear him out, and her refusal to back away from the ugliness in his world had touched his heart. *She'd* touched his heart, cracked it wide open, and in a way that wasn't any good for either of them. But in that moment — sharing his sorry story to someone outside his chain of command for the very first time — he couldn't muster the energy to worry about what was good for them down the road. He could focus only on the now.

"Why the past tense?" she asked.

"Have you ever heard of blast impact?"

"Probably, but pretend like I haven't. Explain it to me," Emilie answered.

"Explosions send out shock waves, which can be very damaging. The closer to the explosion, the greater the impact.

The worst are primary blast injuries, then secondary, tertiary, and quaternary."

"What kinds of injuries?"

"You name it…traumatic brain injuries, sensory damage, hemorrhages, eardrum bursts, organs and bowels bleeding and rupturing. Nothing good."

"And you were in one of these blast impacts?"

"Last spring," Garrett confirmed. "Most of the details are classified, which is fine as I don't remember much of it once the device in the building next to the one we were clearing detonated. Because we were in a relatively small urban space, we experienced multiple shock wave reflections. Mine are considered secondary and tertiary blast injuries. First, the blast wave threw my body. The force broke my back. Unconscious, I landed face down and then—"

Garrett stopped. He'd noticed the continuous stream of tears on Emilie's face. "Keep going," she told him. He tilted his head and looked at her, hating to see such soul-wrenching intensity set in her eyes. "Please."

He sighed audibly, but he did as she asked.

"Shrapnel showered down, slicing through my utilities — that's what we call our uniform," Garrett explained. "And finally, pieces of concrete debris landed on us."

"It's a miracle you lived."

"Maybe, if you believe in that stuff."

"I do." That stiff resolve she showed only when necessary reared its head.

"The surgeons and doctors and nurses and therapists who put me back together like to think they had a hand in it, too."

"And they did! But how do you think surgeons and doctors and nurses and therapists get the determination to do what they do…the ability to conquer *years* of school and studies…the courage to face what they face…the calling to develop those talents and skills? Those are incredible gifts…blessings"

"Touché," Garrett acquiesced with a nod, knowing when he'd been beat.

"How many surgeries?" Emilie asked, not distracted by his wit.

"A lot."

"And therapy?"

"Months."

"Can I see?"

Her request stunned him.

"My back?"

"Yes."

"It's not pretty."

"I'd like to see." She'd shown her moxie all night, and she wasn't backing down then, either.

Garrett shifted on the couch, facing away from Emilie.

After a moment, he gathered up his courage and pulled his undershirt and long-sleeved T-shirt over his head as one. She sat so close that he felt her breath, light with each exhale. Knowing what she saw made his stomach hurt.

Garrett lifted his shirt to put it back on, but Emilie stopped him in his tracks again...

"May I touch you?"

He looked at her over his shoulder, positive he'd misheard her.

"Please?"

She'd already proven he didn't have the ability to tell her no.

"Why would you want to?" Garrett asked.

"My mom says hands hold healing power. She suffered from severe endometriosis, which causes racking abdominal pain. It's nothing compared to what you've been through — *are* going through — but it was a lot for her to endure for many years."

"She's better now?" Garrett asked.

"Yes, she had a hysterectomy, when the pain had become more than she could withstand; it affected every aspect of her day and was destroying her quality of life."

"That's what chronic pain does…chips away at you hour by hour."

"Yes," she agreed. "Mom said that when nothing else worked — not ice packs or pain pills or heating pads — she would ask Dad to set his hands on her stomach. He'd hold her tight, hands flat on her cramping, aching, stricken muscles, and *miraculously*, it would help. Many nights, when she was in a bad way, he'd lay beside her just like that until she relaxed enough to sleep, even if he had to stay there until dawn."

"They have quite a love story."

"Yes," Emilie agreed with an adoring smile.

Garrett set his shirt back on the coffee table and faced away from her once again.

"Go ahead," he said in a raw voice.

Then he held his breath, both hoping for and dreading the feel of her hands on his scarred and puckered skin.

Emilie moved even closer on the couch. Then she flattened one hand against his back. And then the second one.

Her small hands radiated searing heat, or maybe that was just his response to her touch.

Garrett figured she'd lay her hands on him for a minute, a few at the most, and they'd be done with her experiment. But Emilie proved him wrong.

Without an ounce of haste, she set her hands all over his back. She'd place them in one spot, leave them there to warm his flesh, then massage the muscles with gentle strokes before sliding her hands to another spot.

For the first time in months, Garrett didn't feel the rods and screws used to piece him back together. All he felt was Emilie. She filled his senses, replacing the hurt that had become a constant companion since the blast with comfort.

It was almost too much. His breath came rapidly.

A rush of emotion filled his chest.

Garrett squeezed his eyes closed, but still, a tear slid down his face. And then another, and another.

It felt so cathartic that he forgot to be embarrassed.

Then his heart rate slowed to a normal rhythm.

Garrett started relaxing, his head falling forward.

Emilie grabbed two pillows. Leaning into Garrett, she reached around him, stacking the pillows on the arm of the couch in front of him and nudging his forehead to rest on them.

He slumped forward, and still Emilie worked her magic.

She traced his scars and soothed with her gentle touch.

"Does it hurt or help if I massage?"

"Helps," he mumbled into the pillows.

"And can you lay on your stomach?" she asked through the haze or the trance or the spell she'd cast.

"Yes," he sighed.

"Then slide down," she instructed with soft, melodic encouragement, moving off the couch until he'd followed her instructions, repositioned a pillow under his head, and melted into the cushions.

Emilie continued her ministrations, humming or singing under her breath.

Garrett couldn't decipher the words, but he didn't need to know them to benefit from the soothing peace they radiated. He floated in an enlightened state between awareness and oblivion.

Until oblivion won out.

(Be) careful what you wish for.
English idiom used to tell people
to think before they say that
they want something
and to suggest that they may not
actually want it

Garrett woke to the sizzle and smell of bacon cooking.

Had he died and gone to heaven?

Guys like me don't go to heaven.

But he'd just been there, putty in her hands.

Memories flooded back…telling her about the blast, the injuries, the trauma.

He'd expected her to shy away after hearing who and what he was. Or to be disgusted by his scars, both internal and external. He'd been sure she'd stop laying her healing hands upon his back, but she kept going.

Apparently, he'd thanked her selflessness by crashing on her couch.

But he couldn't remember ever sleeping better.

Resisting the urge to stay right where he was, Garrett sat up, then stood.

He stretched, testing his back, and was amazed at the lack of stiffness in it.

Smiling at the Santa fabrics in the quilt she'd draped over him, he folded it up and then put all the throw pillows back where they belonged.

Time to face his angel.

"Good morning," he said, rubbing the back of his neck, suddenly struggling to meet her eyes.

"Good morning," she replied, sunny and warm and sounding totally normal. "Hungry?"

"Always," he confessed, finally lifting his gaze to hers. Her faded blue jeans, grass-stained tennis shoes, and oversized sweatshirt surprised him. She looked ready to tackle a day full of yard work. She'd never been more beautiful to him.

Garrett glanced out the kitchen window to find a snowy wonderland.

"Wow," he exclaimed, moving to take a closer look. "Will they cancel school today?"

"Most likely. I feel a little guilty for not opening the coffee shop, but we're closed on Mondays, and Mr. Moody doesn't believe in wavering from the schedule."

"You'd do things differently?"

"Some things," Emilie admitted, turning off the burner and moving the bacon onto a platter. "I'd keep the nostalgia we all love about the place, but I'd modernize the guest experience." She set the bacon next to a basket of blueberry muffins and poured two cups of coffee before sitting down at the small breakfast table. "And I'd add a roastery."

"A roastery? To process the beans yourself?"

"Exactly." She let out a hopeful, wishful sigh.

"Tell me more," Garrett said, folding a piece of bacon to eat it in one bite and popping it into his mouth.

So she did, describing her dream of purchasing Brew and the empty storefront beside it.

While she shared her vision, Garrett finished off six muffins, more than half the bacon, two tall glasses of milk, and his cup of coffee.

"I'm not always big on faith," Garrett said when she ran out of steam. "But I believe you'll make that goal a reality. And I have faith that you'll get to do it right here in Green Hills."

His encouragement sent a blush to her pretty peaches-and-cream complexion. The sweet look in her eyes and the way she gazed at Garrett tempted him to drag her right back to that comfy couch and spend the day watching movies while snuggled together under her Santa quilt.

It would be so easy. So nice.

But something cautioned Garrett to take it slow. He'd never want to cause her pain, and pain was all he knew. He definitely didn't know if he still had a place with the Raiders, nor if he'd be able to function as a Tier 2 Operator again. And he didn't know if he'd have enough left to give to someone special like Emilie.

"In the meantime, I guess we have a day off." As he said it, he pushed away from the table, still amazed at how little discomfort he had in his back after she'd worked some sort of sorcery on him. He gathered their plates and took them to the sink and turned the water on to warm.

"I figured we'd take your materials list to Jinx to see if he has everything in town," she said, pushing him out of her way with a small hip bump to take over. "I know he'll have the tools we need, and I'm sure he won't mind us borrowing them." She loaded their few items into the dishwasher and washed the skillet and muffin pan. She wiped and dried the counter and folded the cup towel over the oven handle. "He can also recommend some people to help us with the work."

She'd said it with gentle kindness, but she couldn't

completely hide her concern. It warmed his heart that she cared, but it also fed his uncertainty. That vulnerability hurt nearly as much as his injuries. Garrett handled it the way he always did, hiding the hurt and trudging forward.

He moved to stand just a few inches from Emilie. She eyed him wearily and nibbled on her bottom lip, a telltale sign she felt bad — maybe even nervous — about bringing up his issues.

Garrett reached down for her hands, pressing their palms together and entwining their fingers.

"My body was wrecked before I got here. It'll be wrecked when I leave. You have nothing to do with that; *you* aren't causing me pain. And I need you to believe that because I want to do this project. I can't remember the last time I built something for fun…something besides temporary structures for a deployment or mission…something worth putting thought and beauty into. It'll take certain tools to do it right, and it's a multiperson job, so let's visit your friend and see where we go from there."

"Sounds good," Emilie agreed, still a little hesitant but smiling at him again with a gleam in her gaze that did funny things to his insides.

"But we can't go until after I shower," he added. "I appreciate you letting me steal your couch last night." He didn't drop her hands, and his tone grew more heartfelt with every word. "What you did for my back— Emilie, I haven't felt that kind of relief or slept that soundly in a very long time. Thank you."

Emilie nodded. Moisture shimmered in her deep-brown eyes.

Garrett brought their hands to his lips, rolling hers over to brush a kiss over each one. Then he planted one on her forehead and announced he'd be back to get her in less than an hour.

"Thank you for breakfast," he called from the front door

while putting on his boots. He stood, gave Emilie a quick wink, and dashed out the door.

The rest of the day — the entire week, for that matter — flew by.

Jinx Malone turned out to be a lifesaver…and a great guy, so the twinge of jealousy Garrett had experienced when the seniors talked about Jinx being *such a good friend* and *such a big help* to Emilie disappeared upon meeting the man.

He had no call over her and no right to be jealous, anyway.

They'd spent most of the week together, working on the storeroom or prepping for the holiday crush or sharing meals. Throughout it all, Garrett had kept his hands — and his kisses — to himself. Mostly.

There had been one moment Tuesday afternoon when he'd walked into the dining room after the coffee shop had closed for the day, catching her lost in her own thoughts. She'd been wiping down tables and chairs, refilling salt and pepper shakers, and whistling while she worked. He'd stepped back into the shadow to watch her, to memorize how lovely she looked even while doing mindless tasks.

And on Wednesday morning he'd been mighty tempted to plant a big, happy kiss right on Emilie's luscious lips when she exclaimed over the rough-in work he'd done on the storeroom shelving. She'd gone on and on about how sturdy and useful and beautiful the shelves would be, making Garrett feel like a superhero…making him wonder what it would feel like for all that enthusiasm to be focused directly on him. He'd settled for wrapping her in a big bear hug, squeezing until she couldn't stop laughing and feeling the silkiness of her hair against his lips with a soft kiss to the top of her head before releasing her from the comical hug. But, man, had he yearned for a real kiss.

Then, on Thursday night after a long day at the coffee shop, there'd been a moment, the kind that deserves capital letters, one fraught with chemistry, like a live wire sizzling between them. The day had been more exhausting than usual because a tour bus on a holiday shopping excursion had broken down in town. The tourists needed places to stay out of the cold, so Emilie had overridden Mr. Moody's authority and kept Brew open until their transportation had been repaired. She had run to the Get'n'Go grocery store for ingredients to make chicken spaghetti, which she served to every single member of the travel group. She'd defrosted three chocolate cakes from the freezer and dusted them with powdered sugar for dessert. He'd lost count of the number of questions Emilie had asked to distract the worried individuals, conversations she'd shared, and pots of coffee she'd brewed throughout the day.

She was spectacular.

Braving the cold, they'd waved goodbye to their new friends from outside the coffee shop entrance as the bus drove away. Without thinking, Garrett had lowered his arm around Emilie, tucking her into his side to shield her from the icy wind. She'd responded by cuddling as close as possible and huddling her head close to his chest.

"I'm so tired," she confessed with a dramatic moan, lifting her face from the cocoon he'd formed around her.

She'd said it with an easy smile, but when their eyes locked, the air around them sparked.

The Moment.

Emilie had grasped the edges of his unzipped coat and gently tugged as she rose on her tiptoes.

"Thank you," she said. Her voice came out deeper than usual. It sent tingles down Garrett's spine. "I couldn't have made it through the day without your help."

Then Emilie had pulled him toward her and placed a tender kiss on his lips.

As fast as it happened, it was over.

She released his coat, stepped past him, and went inside to lock up for the night.

They'd said good night and gone their separate ways, but Garrett hadn't stopped thinking about that kiss.

A peck, really.

Nothing romantic about it, Garrett told himself on repeat.

She'd rested her closed lips against his closed lips.

No big deal.

Yeah, right.

Eager to work on the storeroom project, Garrett arrived at the coffee shop a little before 6:00 a.m. on Friday — well before it opened for the day. On his way through the front door, he glowered at the mistletoe hanging right above where they'd been standing at the exact moment she'd kissed him.

Part of him wished it hadn't happened.

He'd be leaving soon. Emilie might also leave soon. They'd formed a fine friendship and enjoyed one another's company. It didn't need to be more than that.

Sure, she was gorgeous. And sweet and kind. She liked to cook, and Garrett liked to eat, so naturally, he enjoyed eating whatever she cooked for him. The way she fussed over their meals was cute. She was cute. And she had such a good heart. When he wanted to set Mr. Moody straight, she always responded with patience. She doted on those seniors as if every one of them was her beloved grandparent. She knew each of her customers and their families. She really was the perfect definition of the *small-town girl next door*.

The thought made him laugh. Emilie made him laugh. And think. And want.

The part of him that wanted her — and he wanted her on

every level: her heart, her soul, her spirit, her attention, her everything — that part of him wished he'd taken advantage of the mistletoe. Garrett wished he'd tightened his arms around her, trapping hers between them. He wished he had lowered his mouth to hers a second time, taking charge and kissing her properly. He wished a lot of things.

But wishing and wanting paved a path to pain — pain neither of them needed.

He shot another hateful glance at the bouquet and, with the key she'd given him to come and go as he wanted to work on the storeroom, unlocked the front door. He didn't bother with the lights, still grumbling about plants and pretty girls as he walked through the dining room and into the kitchen, where Emilie stood stirring something in a massive metal mixing bowl.

She yelped and jumped a mile in the air, losing her grip on the bowl.

Garrett's soldier's instinct of fight over flight took charge. In a heartbeat, he was by Emilie's side, catching the bowl, and steadying her.

He even disarmed her.

"Really?" he asked, taking the wooden spoon from her hand, which she brandished like a hammer. "*That* was going to protect you?" he teased.

Emilie flattened her lips, obviously trying to suppress a fit of giggles.

"What are you doing here?" she asked. Her eyes danced with joy.

"I could ask you the same thing."

Emilie snatched her mixing bowl and went for her spoon.

Garrett held it above his head. He lifted an eyebrow, indicating she wasn't getting what she wanted until he got an answer.

She folded her arms with a faux pout. The glow in her

cheeks and laughter still fighting for release promised she wasn't truly put out with him.

He didn't budge.

"I'm using the kitchen before Byron arrives."

"Why?"

"I told you the other day…sometimes I need to bake, and it's just easier to avoid dealing with the lord of the kitchen. Now may I have my spoon?"

"What are you making?" he asked, dropping his hand, but not handing over the spoon just yet.

"Rice Krispie Treats," she answered, swiping the spoon from him. Only because he let her, and they both knew it.

"Don't they sell those at the store?"

"They aren't the same." Her aggressive stirring emphasized her know-it-all tone. Garrett was having a blast with this side of Emilie's spunk.

"They look the same. Same blue packaging…same three elves."

"I guess store-bought is fine in a pinch, but homemade is better," she said, setting a catering-sized rectangular cake pan beside the bowl on the prep table.

"Because…" he said, fishing for more just to keep her talking with such animated passion.

"Because store-bought tastes like chemicals."

When Emilie started dumping cereal-and-marshmallow mixture into the pan, Garrett picked up the bowl and held it upside down over the pan. Without a word, Emilie accepted his help and began scraping the contents from the bowl. Then she took a spatula, rubbed it with butter, and began flattening the mixture in the pan.

A small amount of the mixture remained stuck to the spoon. Instead of using the greased spatula to add it to the pan, Emilie pulled the leftover mixture off with her fingers.

"Cereal, marshmallows, and a quarter-cup of margarine.

That's all you need…no added preservatives," she told him as she lifted her fingers to his lips. "Here, see for yourself."

She played with fire, and she knew it because her cheeks flamed a fetching salmon shade of pink. But she didn't back down.

Neither did Garrett.

Wrapping his hand around her wrist, he moved his mouth to her offering. Her pulse beneath his fingers picked up speed. Yes, Emilie felt the attraction and the magnetic pull and the magic between them just as fiercely as Garrett did.

She swallowed and lifted her chin. Garrett relished her obstinate spirit.

Slowly, he tasted the Rice Krispie Treat, taking his time to savor the feel of her fingertips against his lips. Before releasing her arm, he slid his mouth to her wrist and placed a kiss on her thrumming heartbeat.

"You're right," he said, eyes locked on hers. "Delicious."

"Yes, well—" Emilie pulled her arm from his grasp and lifted her nose a little higher in the air. "I told you so." Then she twirled away from him and moved to a safe distance. Garrett couldn't help but chuckle.

Did I win or lose that little battle of wills?

He licked marshmallow from his lips and watched Emilie measure ingredients for another batch of treats. She flounced around the kitchen, dutifully ignoring his presence, although color still bloomed on her face.

Won, for sure.

12

"What are these for?" Garrett asked, holding yet another bowl of cereal mixture for Emilie to spread into another pan. They had a system: While she measured cereal and melted marshmallows, Garrett prepped to work on the storeroom. When Emilie called him, he came to hold the bowl for her. Then they'd do it again.

"The football team, band, cheerleaders, trainers, student managers, and equipment kids."

"So basically," he teased. "The entire school?"

"Basically," she agreed with a giggle. "There's a playoff game tonight; these are for the pep rally."

"How many more do you need?"

"With what I made yesterday, this batch puts us over three hundred. That'll be plenty."

"And what time is the pep rally?"

"This afternoon. It's a send-off before the team leaves for the out-of-town game, so I'll close up after lunch to take these to the school."

"Mr. Moody doesn't mind?"

"Oh, no, everything will close," she said, taking the spoon, spatula, and mixing bowl to the sink. Garrett followed with the cooled stockpot she'd used to melt marshmallows.

"Everything?"

"Of course. For the game." She said it as if shutting every business in town for a high school football game happened regularly.

"And are you going to the game?"

"Of course," she repeated. "It's a long drive, but would you like to go with me?"

He didn't have time to answer. Byron entered the kitchen and instantly bellowed about the mess and the pans and decried the audacity of some people and the pathetic working conditions he had to endure.

Garrett got out of there as fast as he could, sequestering himself in the storeroom and solitary bliss.

He lost all track of time hanging cleats, to which he'd attach the wooden units. Reinforced that way, the shelves wouldn't sway under the weight of everything Emilie hoped to organize on them.

"How's it going in here?" she asked from the doorway.

"All done," he confirmed, driving in the last screw. "At least for this step of the process."

"This is so professional," she said, walking over to run a hand over what he'd built. "Nothing like the wobbly metal contraptions I buy at the big box store and pray won't fall on someone."

"These won't fall," Garrett told her with zero doubt.

"I'm sure they won't," she agreed with awe. "I can't believe this is real; it's going to be so nice…and beautiful," she added, stroking his ego without even knowing it. Garrett wanted to strut like a rooster. "I'll never be able to repay you."

"You could buy me a hot chocolate at the game."

"You want to go?"

"It sounds like going is my only dinner option, if the entirety of Green Hills will be there."

"I mean, you're welcome to the peanut butter, jelly, and sliced bread at my house."

Garrett pretended to consider his options. He liked flirting with her. He especially liked how she got a little feisty when she flirted back.

Warning bells sounded in the recesses of his conscience. Flirting and teasing led to things he couldn't give. If she'd tried to hide her budding feelings for him, she'd failed miserably. The way she looked at him spoke volumes. The warmth in her eyes promised a devotion he'd not believed existed. At least not until that week with Emilie.

"You should know, though — before you decide — we're stopping on the way for the best chicken-fried steak and mashed potatoes north of Fort Worth."

"Well," he said, ignoring those warning bells. "In that case, I *have* to go."

*T*hree hours later, Garrett had attended his first Green Hills High School pep rally, helped distribute more than three hundred snack bags, met what felt like a thousand people, and enjoyed the best chicken-fried steak and mashed potatoes he'd ever eaten…just as Emilie had promised.

"I'm starting to understand the draw of small towns," he

told her, driving down a remote farm-to-market road in search of a football stadium located miles outside another tiny community, two hours from Green Hills. With the snow and freezing temperatures, he'd convinced Emilie to let him drive his truck, which was better equipped for the elements with four-wheel drive and a heavier body. As always, their conversations had come easily; he'd let her do most of the talking, simply enjoying her stories and how much she delighted in retelling them. Both their arms rested on the center console, relaxed as they went, and Garrett fought the urge to tangle his fingers with hers.

"You didn't grow up in one?"

"Sorry to say I'm a big-city boy."

"Did you play sports in school?"

"Some," he answered. "But not like this, not with the support of an entire town. I've never carried a whole community's hopes on my shoulders." He cast her a teasing glance.

"We're not that bad," she said, only half-heartedly defending the passionate Wolf Pack fans who had been at the send-off pep rally, cheering with pride. From the high school to the restaurant and along the highway, it had been a steady caravan of Green Hills' faithful.

"I don't know," he joked. "I'm guessing they're pretty rowdy once the game starts."

"I suppose we are," she said cryptically.

"*We?* Do you lose your cool and become a raving fanatic once they kick off?"

"I wouldn't say I'm quiet," she admitted, almost shyly.

Garrett laughed out loud. He couldn't wait.

"Garrett, you're wrong about one thing, though." The intention in her voice raised the hairs on the back of his neck. He looked over to find that look of adoration shining in her eyes again. His heart skipped a beat.

"What about?" he asked, less than impressed to hear the rawness in his voice.

"You carry the hopes of an entire nation on your back, and you make us very proud."

Garrett's throat thickened. When words failed him, he did what he'd wanted to do all along, covering her hand with his much larger one, holding on to an angel while he could.

*G*arrett did the same on the way home, except his angel had worn herself out cheering her team to victory.

He'd had as much fun watching her yell at referees, cringe at tackles, and go crazy for touchdowns as he had watching the actual game. The two teams were evenly matched, so the score was tight with the lead changing sides throughout all four quarters. When the Green Hills Wolf Pack intercepted a pass with less than a minute left to secure the win, Emilie had totally lost it, jumping and screaming and crying and hugging. Garrett had enjoyed that part, too.

They'd barely left the stadium parking lot when her adrenaline crashed. Garrett had reached into the back seat to grab a blanket he always left there in the winter. He set it on the console between them as an invitation. In less than sixty seconds, Emilie had curled into a ball without releasing her seat belt and laid down her head.

With a quiet drive back to Green Hills looming, Garrett turned on the radio and found a classic country station, keeping the volume low enough not to wake her. Then he reached into the back seat again for his coat. One-handed, he draped it over Emilie and gently pulled the length of her hair from underneath the makeshift throw before smoothing wayward tendrils from her face. He indulged, letting the blonde silk slide through his fingers.

When a deep tug of yearning — for her, for a future, for a *them* — filled his chest, he dropped the strands. With a stern self-reprimand, Garrett intended to drive with both hands on the wheel. But he couldn't quite do it and settled for resting his hand on her shoulder.

He pulled into her driveway two hours later and squeezed her arm.

"We're here," he said softly.

No response.

Garrett killed the engine, climbed out, and walked around to her side. He opened it, and she shivered, grumbling at the cold air he let in.

Giving up, Garrett dug in her purse for her keys, walked to open the front door and turned on a light in her living room. Then he walked back out to the truck, unclicked her seat belt, and lifted Emilie into his arms.

She responded by curling into his chest, and Garrett felt like the king of the world, despite the gripping pain in his back caused by carrying her.

He figured he owed her for tucking him in when he'd fallen asleep on her couch, and he certainly didn't mind repaying the debt.

Finding the master bedroom at the end of the hall, Garrett balanced Emilie in his arms to turn on a bedside lamp and pull back her quilts and covers. He laid her on the mattress, unlaced her boots, and slid them off. He worried she'd be too hot in the multiple layers she still wore from the game, but she didn't seem to mind.

One couldn't help but admire the way she'd slept through the whole ritual, like a child at complete ease with the world. Garrett liked that she felt safe enough with him to embrace such peace.

He watched her sleep for a minute, too beautiful for him to look away.

God, what would I give to have the right to kick off my own boots and climb in beside her, to tuck her close, and hold her all night?

Garrett ran the back of his fingers down her cheek and got out of there.

Walking away was getting too hard.

13

You've always got to have a plan B.
You've got to be able to shift gears and
find a new course of action.
Joe Teti

*E*milie's Saturday didn't leave a single free second to feel bad or embarrassed about falling asleep — and staying that way — after the game the night before.

From the moment she'd unlocked the front door, Brew had been slammed.

Teens celebrating the game, and old-timers reliving a lifetime of them, filled every inch of the dining room. They filtered out only to be replaced by holiday shoppers in search of a pick-me-up between stores. Once they moved on, the regulars moved in to reclaim their space, irritated they'd had to share it all day. As a collective, they kept Emilie and Byron and their part-time weekend help hopping.

Emilie hadn't sat down once all day, and she'd been unable to close the coffee shop until almost two hours later than the times listed on the door. In a mild stupor, she let muscle memory take over to clean. With all the chores done, she slid on her coat and scarf, grabbed her purse, and checked appliances one last time to make sure everything had been turned off. Desperate to go home and collapse, Emilie ventured back to the storeroom to check on Garrett.

He wasn't there. A note on a napkin explained with a brief, incomplete sentence: *gone to Malone's – G.*

Emilie examined his handwriting — all three words of it. Dark pencil marks, meticulous print, and right to the point…so reflective of the man. She grinned and tucked the napkin into her bag.

Then she studied the work he'd accomplished so far. It looked amazing. Garrett had installed the side panels of the shelving units and finished framing the cleaning supply closet. Emilie marveled at how quickly the project progressed. It was really coming together. The design appeared flawless, putting every inch to good use without cramping the space. What a talent Garrett possessed.

A piece of Garrett lived in the workmanship; when she ran a hand over the wooden structures, Emilie felt his presence there. In the future, she'd think of him every time she walked into the storeroom. Would those thoughts bring with them sadness or a smile? Both, most likely.

She couldn't see him staying. His back injuries might not allow for the same type of missions and operations he'd done previously, but Emilie suspected the Marines had other vital roles for Garrett to fill. For that matter, she had no idea how the military worked. He probably didn't have a choice in the matter either way, not until his enlistment was up.

And what then?

Emilie didn't doubt she could fall in love with Garrett Banks quite easily.

You're already halfway there, her conscience whispered.

She'd known the man for a week, but she'd been waiting for his arrival her entire life.

Not one to date much in high school and college, she'd been content with casual outings with friends. There'd been a few cute boys along the way, but none who made her heart skip beats and her skin tingle the way Garrett did. From the moment she looked up to find him sitting at the coffee bar, she'd sensed he'd be the one…the hero in her love story…the prince in her fairy tale.

But life wasn't a fairy tale, and while Garrett was most definitely a hero, he wasn't hers to have.

Her Christmas wish hadn't changed. She'd do her best to ensure he had a beautiful visit to Green Hills, that he had fun with his woodworking project, and that he remembered to smile a little more from time to time.

And she'd do all she could to protect her heart along the way.

An affable yet melancholy mood fell over Emilie.

Convinced it was merely exhaustion making her feel gloomy, she turned off the lights and headed home.

*H*er softest sweats, thickest cozy socks, tomato soup, and a gooey grilled cheese sandwich lifted her spirits a bit. Listening to Bing Crosby sing Christmas classics did wonders, too.

Spiral notebook in hand to work on her holiday to-do list, Emilie settled on the couch in a much better frame of mind. She'd just arranged a quilt over her folded legs when the doorbell rang.

"Come in," she called out.

"Why is your door unlocked?" Garrett asked by way of *hello.*

"Because I haven't gone to bed yet," she answered, way too happy to see him.

"It's 9:30 at night," he argued.

"In Green Hills," Emilie added.

He couldn't dispute that fact. But he did grumble, "Lock your door," while closing it behind him.

"Did you eat?" she asked, admiring the view as he shrugged out of his coat and removed one boot and then the other.

"Yeah, with Jinx Malone, actually. At the Three-Toed Turtle."

"*Ahh*, Triple T's. Did you have a strawberry milkshake?"

"It's twenty-seven degrees outside," he pointed out.

"*Sooo?*"

"I passed on the ice cream." He shook his head at Emilie, half-laughing at her drama. "But the food was pretty outstanding."

"Earl runs a tight ship and serves a mean burger and fries," she said with respect.

"Did you know Jinx and Matthias Noble were like brothers?"

"Inseparable throughout their entire childhood," Emilie confirmed. "Matty's sudden departure really hurt Jinx and his grandfather, Duke."

"Yeah, we talked about him, too." Garrett's eyes ping-ponged between the couch and the chair adjacent to it and back again. After a silent tug-of-war, he chose the chair.

Emilie's hopes deflated a smidge, but she didn't let it show.

"Duke's a very sweet man." She smiled, thinking of the many Saturday mornings that she and her dad had spent at Duke's hardware store when she was a little kid. The men would talk through projects and gossip in equal measure. Emilie would stuff herself with popcorn, always hot and fresh with the perfect amount of salt and butter from the red self-serve popper on wheels. Jinx had done a wonderful job with the shop after Duke's Alzheimer's diagnosis, but it wasn't the same without Duke there every day.

"Jinx gave up everything to come back here to take care of Duke — a basketball career, his plans to continue college for a second degree, his life in Houston — *everything.*"

"It must've been a very difficult choice," Emilie said.

"Not according to Jinx. He said there was no decision to make." Garrett studied the rug under his feet while he spoke. "He loves his grandpa and wanted to be here for him. The end."

"Switching gears is never that simple. I applaud Jinx for making a life for himself here once he came home — he's made the hardware store his own, and you wouldn't believe the furniture he makes on the side. But I don't believe for a second that being the primary caregiver for a loved one with dementia, that watching the disease rob them of their lifestyle and abilities, or that walking away from the plan Jinx had for his life was easy."

"No, I guess not." Garrett finally lifted his gaze to meet her scrutinizing eyes.

They weren't talking *only* about Jinx.

"I'm glad y'all had dinner," Emilie said, forcing a lighter tone into her voice. "The storeroom—"

"I need to go," Garrett said at the same time she'd spoken.

"Okay," she allowed with thoughtful intention. He obviously had a lot on his mind. "Would you like to go to church with me tomorrow morning?"

A crease in his brow showed his mental tug-of-war had reconvened.

"I appreciate the offer, but I'd better keep working at Brew."

It was a cop-out, and they both knew it.

"No problem," she said, letting him off the hook with

pleasant patience. "I just wanted you to know you're always invited."

Emilie's eyes tracked Garrett as he stood, walked to the front door, then walked back to the couch and reached out a hand toward her. He looked at her expectantly, so she put down her pen and paper and laid her hand in his.

Garrett pulled her to her feet, and Emilie set her quilt to the side.

With her in tow, Garrett returned to the door, shoved his feet in his boots and his arms in his coat.

"Lock it," he instructed.

Then he kissed her on top of the head and walked out.

14

If you love something, set it free.
If it comes back, it's yours.
If not, it was never meant to be.
Popular saying of unknown origin

$\mathcal{E}$milie didn't see Garrett on Sunday or Monday.

She'd attended church Sunday morning and then gone to her parents' house for lunch with her family. She'd stayed there watching football with her brother for much of the afternoon. When she got home, she hauled Christmas decorations from her attic and had a ball revisiting the stories and memories behind every treasured item as she transformed her house for the season.

With Brew closed on Monday, she'd spent the day with the Christmas Eve Festival committee, which they'd roped her into under duress — two years ago. In all honesty, she loved being part of it every December. They'd walked a new parade route, scouting for potential issues before they arose. They worked on logistics, confirmed booth rentals, distributed time slots for unloading, arranged animals for the live nativity scene, went over details with Santa, and prepared an event checklist for local businesses and visiting vendors. It took all day, but what they had accomplished thrilled the committee.

For the coffee shop's part, on top of their regular business hours at Brew, which wouldn't change during the festival, Emilie had agreed to set up a coffee station next to Steep's booth. Together, they'd provide coffee and tea, of course, but also hot chocolate, wassail, and water. Both businesses had curated gift bundles of coffees, teas, branded mugs and thermoses, and T-shirts and sweatshirts with cute coffee-addict sayings.

All those "extras" meant more to-dos on Emilie's list.

Midmorning on Tuesday, she stood at the coffee counter double-checking said list, scribbling details she might forget in the chaos and adding even more bullet points as she thought of things that also needed doing.

"Whoa!" declared a woman sitting at a table close by. Emilie heard her but didn't pay attention to the odd exclamation.

"Oh my," she heard someone else say in a breathy voice.

"I think he's looking for you, dear," Blythe Asher said, nudging Emilie in the ribs as she slid behind the counter to steal a scone.

Emilie looked at her in confusion.

Then she followed Blythe's silent instruction to look to the entryway.

Oh my was right.

Garrett — clean-shaven and looking very serious — in Dress Blues stopped her heart.

Then, at the thought he must be leaving, it started beating in a frantic, out-of-control rhythm. She couldn't catch her breath and blinked at a ridiculous rate to push back the hazy darkness invading her peripheral vision.

A plethora of medals hung from bright ribbons in various

colors and stripes, creating a pop of contrast against the red-trimmed, midnight-navy jacket that fit his form to perfection. A thick red band ran down his blue pants from hip to ankle. One could see their reflection in the shine of his black shoes. He'd tucked his hat and a laptop computer under one arm. The whole uniform might've been tailored just for Garrett.

More accurately, he'd been made to wear it.

"Is everything okay?" she asked when he walked to the coffee counter, forgetting to say *hi* first.

"I have a meeting," he said with clipped, concise words.

"That's why you're in uniform?"

"Yes, I thought I'd use the Wi-Fi here, but…"

"There are too many people here; it's so loud," she said, finishing his sentence. "The library — just around the corner. It's a school day, so things should be relatively quiet. You can use a dedicated study room away from the multipurpose areas, just in case there are groups meeting there this morning. The librarian, Nathan Quinn, can help. He'll get you logged on in no time."

Relief flooded Garrett's features.

"Go outside, turn right, and keep walking away from the courthouse square. Turn right at the light, and the library is a full block down on your left…right next to the Redbud Park entrance. You can't miss it," she said, her tone full of encouragement.

"Thank you," he said with a nod before pivoting on his heel.

"Garrett," Emilie called out, stopping him as he opened the door. He turned around to look at her, and Emilie desperately wished she could read the thoughts whirling behind his stormy eyes. Her stomach fluttered, but she had to know… "Will you come back?" she asked. "To the shop, I mean."

"It could take a while," he replied, not saying *no,* but not quite promising to return, either.

"I'll wait," she stated. "I'll wait as long as you need."

And she would. Emilie decided then and there as she watched him go in purposeful strides: Garrett Banks was worth waiting for.

"*Woo-wee,*" Alora Johnson whistled. "He's like a book boyfriend who jumped right off the pages of a good romance novel, come to life just like Pinocchio."

"If you'll recall, Pinocchio got himself into a world of trouble," someone said, apparently enjoying the show from the peanut gallery.

"I'm guessing he's past that section of the story," another voice from another table added.

"Yep, and ready for the redemption part," Alora agreed. "Emilie, if you don't pluck that boy off the market, I just might rethink my policy on younger men," she hollered from the corner table on the far side of the room, making sure everyone heard her word for word.

"I would if I could," Emilie said in a soft whisper that *no one* else could hear.

I would if I could, she thought again for good measure.

*E*ven though she'd seen him in his formal uniform, knew what to expect, and had braced herself for the impact, Emilie's jittering nerves switched into overdrive when Garrett walked through the coffee shop's front door several hours later. He really was *beyond* handsome.

Emilie stopped folding Brew sweatshirts to give him her full attention.

Be supportive, no matter what he says.

"I still have a pot of coffee on; would you like a cup?"

"Nah, I better not. It's a pain to get stains out if I accidentally get something on this. But thanks," he said.

"I've already cleaned the counter if you'd like to set down your hat."

"My cover," he said with a sweet smile.

"I'm sorry?" she asked, completely lost.

"We call our hats *covers*," he explained as he placed the object on the bar.

His lips still curved in a hint of a grin. He spoke in a light-hearted tone. Even his eyes held a playful gleam.

But his jaw remained clenched, and his shoulders remained stiff. It — something — wasn't good.

"You need a tree," Garrett said.

"Do what?" Emilie asked, failing to keep up.

"I noticed all your Christmas decorations. They're wonderful. But you don't have a tree at your house."

She'd assembled and decorated the artificial tree that went in Brew's front window every year, but Garrett was right; Emilie enjoyed having a real tree at home, and she hadn't found time to pick one for her living room.

"You saw my decorations?"

Garrett pulled two keys from his pocket, laid them on the counter, and slid them her way.

"This morning," he admitted. "While you were here, I changed the door handles and locks at your house."

"Today?" Emilie stammered. "You broke into my house *today*?"

Garrett had the decency to grimace with guilt. But he didn't apologize.

"It took me less than fifteen seconds. Those locks were trash." He shrugged. "Now you have new ones, with a keypad and an app for remote entry." He paused, visibly gauging her reaction. In response, Emilie just eyed him. "But now you need a tree," he continued. "Your decorations are too beautiful to be missing a tree."

Flattery will get you everywhere, she thought. But Emilie wasn't quite ready to let him off the hook.

"Do I have a code to get into my own house?"

"You do, and those keys are backup."

"Well, what is it?"

"1201," he answered. "The day we met."

That took the wind right out of her sails.

"Thank you," she said, conceding appreciation for his thoughtful gesture. The old handles *were* in bad shape, and it would be nice to have keyless entry and an app to let family and friends in if they stopped before she got home.

"You're welcome," Garrett said back. Emilie ignored the thrill of victory shining all over his face. "Now, where do we get a tree?"

"We'll have to go tomorrow," Emilie told him. "The youth group at one of the churches runs a nice tree lot, but it's only open Wednesday through Saturday."

"We'll go after you close the coffee shop?" he asked.

"That sounds perfect," she answered.

"It's a date," Garrett announced.

Those three little words — only eight letters in total — played through Emilie's mind the rest of the afternoon and evening. They haunted her sleep that night. They wreaked havoc on her while she attempted to be productive at work on Wednesday.

It's just a saying. But it could be a date. Or simply an outing. Just a friend helping a friend select a Christmas tree. But it could be a date…a real date.

The debate going on in her head refused to shush.

For Garrett's part, he didn't seem to have a worry in the world.

After he'd proclaimed they had a date planned, he'd run to his hotel room to change out of his uniform and into work clothes, returned to Brew, and worked on the storeroom — possibly all night long, if judging by the amount of progress he'd made. The wooden structures looked complete, and he'd painted the cleaning closet.

When Emilie got to the shop early Wednesday morning, he'd already arrived and started sanding and trimming the shelving units.

Minutes after she'd flipped the *Open* sign for the day, Jinx and one of his employees came in, accepted cups of coffee, and disappeared into the storeroom with Garrett.

Wondering about what they were doing did nothing to calm her jitteriness. But three bodies in the storeroom would be tight enough, and Emilie didn't want to be in the way.

So, she served coffee and pastries and watched the clock. She wrapped holiday gift bundles for the festival and counted the seconds as they ticked by in slow motion. And when Mr. Moody complained it was five minutes past closing and everyone needed to go home...for once, Emilie agreed. She turned the sign on the door back to *Closed*, cleaned tables while guests still sat at them, and even took Mr. Moody's coffee cup away to wash before he'd swallowed the last swig.

She'd taken one step toward the storeroom when all three men walked out of it. They closed the door behind them, set the coffee cups and lunch plates they'd used throughout the day in the kitchen sink, and told Emilie bye with kind yet conspiratorial smiles. At the front door, Garrett called over his shoulder, "I'm running to the hotel to shower. Then I'll pick you up at your house. We're going on a tree hunt."

A tree hunt?

We're going on a tree hunt?

"Are we kindergartners?" Emilie grumbled to herself, standing in her closet at home, changing into a pair of blue jeans and layering a heavy cable-knit sweater over a long-sleeved thermal and a brown plaid flannel button-up. "Just like little boys…they hide in their playhouse all day long and then expect everyone to be ready at their whimsy," she grumbled some more in front of the bathroom mirror, touching up her makeup and brushing her long hair until the sunlight filtering through the window made it shine. The doorbell rang right when she finished applying her favorite peach lip gloss. She surveyed her reflection and decided she looked quite nice. *Take that, soldier boy.*

Emilie opened the front door to discover that Garrett looked quite nice, too. *Quite* nice.

He, too, had on blue jeans. Garrett normally wore some style of work pants, sometimes in camo prints and sometimes in solid colors, which definitely looked good on him. But his muscular frame did something else to denim. His ever-present white undershirt showed at the open *V* of a thick quarter-zip pullover, also filled out just right in the shoulders, chest, and arms, so there was no doubt of the muscles underneath. He'd traded his black military-style boots for a pair of brown cowboy boots.

Yeah…far beyond "quite nice."

Emilie blushed at the thought and hoped Garrett would assume the blast of cold air caused the rise of color in her face.

"You could've let yourself in," she told him, teasing him about knowing the code while grabbing her coat and scarf from the chair beside the door.

"Nah," he replied with a smile that said he still didn't feel bad at all about breaking into her house and changing her locks. "This is your house."

"Garrett, you're always welcome here." She'd dropped the playful tone in her voice to make sure he understood she meant it.

"Thank you, angel."

"Angel?" she echoed.

"Since the day we met," he confirmed, typing the code into the keypad to lock the door.

Then he grabbed her hand to hold while they walked down the snowy drive to his truck.

Garrett held her hand in his as they meandered through the Christmas tree lot, too. He charmed her, pulling her from tree to tree like a kid in a candy store... *What about this one, or maybe one bigger? Or how about that one? No, it needs to be fatter.*

He seemed lighter, like some of the tension he carried around had eased. Garrett still didn't divulge personal stuff as they talked, but he shared more of himself in other ways. He laughed more, and he smiled more...showed affection more naturally, like holding her hand or slinging his arm over her shoulders as they examined trees. When he saw the snow angels kids had made on the hill beside the tree lot, he demanded they make some. And then he'd gently brushed the snow from her coat and hair when they stood to admire their work. He'd even kissed Emilie on the nose *after* pinging her with a snowball, apologizing with a half-hearted claim that when he saw her standing there, backlit in the last golden ray of the setting sun, he just couldn't resist.

She giggled at his antics and delighted in his attention. Emilie wouldn't have minded in the least if that evening could've lasted forever.

His playful mood lasted until later that night, until after they'd set up her perfect tree, created a perfect pizza picnic in the glow of the twinkle lights they'd strung on the tree, and snuggled on the couch watching *It's a Wonderful Life*, the perfect classic Christmas movie.

"I can't drive you to the football game on Saturday," Garrett said, holding her hand at the front door…ending her perfect date. "I'm sorry, angel," he added, looking at their entwined fingers, rubbing his thumb over her skin as though memorizing the feel.

"When do you leave?" Emilie asked past a lump in her throat.

Garrett lifted his head to meet her gaze. Regret — or maybe it was more accurately described as remorse — filled his eyes and clenched his jaw.

"Friday morning."

An invisible force struck Emilie, causing her shoulders to slump in a reflexive action to protect her heart. Her expression crumbled. She understood a tiny inkling of the trauma Garrett's body sustained in that blast wave.

Garrett's expression turned to one of misery. He shook his head once and pulled Emilie close, folding her into his chest and wrapping his arms around her like a steel trap.

Emilie trembled, but she didn't cry. She'd be sure to thank the Lord for that strength later.

She did, however, try to absorb and commit to memory *everything* about that hug…Garrett's scent, his heat, the feel of his body sheltering hers in a storm. To make it through the coming months, she'd need to recall the details — to revisit that moment — because getting over Garrett would not be easy.

Eventually, he loosened his hold and looked down at Emilie. His hands moved to frame her face and cup her jaw. His fingers tangled in her long hair, heating the back of her neck. Then he ducked his head, lowered his lips to hers, and gave her something much better to remember.

15

I love cafe culture, art and intellect,
the long hello and sweet goodbye.
Melody Gardot

ears still didn't come that night.

They couldn't. Emilie could only handle one earth-shattering emotion at a time, and after that kiss, euphoria trumped all else.

She'd clung to him, and he'd kept kissing.

If the devil had dared to deal in that moment, there was no telling what she'd have bargained to freeze time.

Sadly, or perhaps luckily, he hadn't. Once Garrett had thoroughly and completely knocked her socks off with *The Kiss*, he'd said good night and gone to his hotel, promising to see her in just a few hours at the coffee shop.

Standing in a daze at her kitchen sink the next morning, Emilie admired the sun rising over the horizon. She applauded God's artwork, the way the soft, buttery light spread hope and resurgence like strokes from a paintbrush. A new day… What promised to be a difficult one, but one she'd determined to make the most of. If it was her last day with Garrett, she wouldn't waste it.

With that thought, Emilie lifted her fingers to her lips; they still tingled from Garrett's kiss. She grinned, relishing the feeling.

Whistling and humming and singing, she showered and dressed for the day, drove to work, and unlocked the back door. When she opened it, a harsh odor assaulted her senses and turned her stomach. Wood stain.

"Garrett?" Emilie called out.

"Hey," he greeted, coming out of the storeroom wearing a wide, boyish smile. "Sorry about the smell. It'll be pretty rank for a day or two. Three at the worst. I hope," he added with a sheepish shrug.

"What are you doing?"

"We finished the remodel," he said. Joy danced in his eyes, and she couldn't look away.

"Morning, Em," Jinx called from inside the storeroom.

With her wide-eyed gaze glued to Garrett, Emilie strode forward to see for herself.

Before he moved aside to let her pass, Garrett lifted her chin with a caress and placed a tender kiss on her lips.

"Hi," he whispered.

Emilie's heart did somersaults.

"What do you think?" Garrett asked, stepping out of the doorway to reveal the most magnificent restaurant storage room ever created.

She gaped at the beautiful dark-stained shelving units, some wide open for larger equipment and some divided into cubbies for tall cookie sheets and bakeware. Those at eye level had stair-stepped inserts for cans and dry ingredients. Runners on the next level down turned the shelves into open drawers, making it convenient to access items at the back. A light glowed from the cleaning closet, which someone had stocked and organized to perfection. An antique board with *Brew* painted across it in swooping letters hung on the outside wall of the closet; beneath the board, the same repurposed wood had been used to create a coat or apron rack with small, locker-like openings above each hook. Next to that, the same wood was cut and mitered, forming a stunning frame for a black-and-white picture of Roanna, standing at the coffee counter and beaming at the photographer behind the camera.

The tears finally came.

"The back door?" Emilie asked past her emotions. So many emotions!

"Yeah," Garrett confessed, almost shyly. "Merry Christmas," he added.

It was too much to process: meeting him, getting to know him, working together, his determination to remodel the storeroom, his beautiful design coming to fruition, his gift, the way he understood her, the way she loved him.

I love him.

Not knowing what else to do, Emilie threw herself into his embrace and held on for dear life.

"Thank you," she cried. "Thank you so much."

"Your boy here's got real talent," Jinx said, elbowing Garrett like they'd been friends for years.

"How in the world did you get all this done?" Emilie asked, easing from Garrett's arms to dry her cheeks. "I mean, look at everything," she added, turning circles to take it all in. "It's incredible!"

"As a very wise angel suggested, I got some great help," Garrett said with a nod at Jinx.

"It was my pleasure," Jinx assured them. "Grandad loved this place...spent many hours sitting at Miss Roanna's counter, sipping coffee and chatting with friends. He'd love that you honored her with this project."

"Go grab a stool now, and I'll bring you both breakfast. I'd say you've more than earned it."

"I'm not one to turn down a good meal," Jinx joked, leading the way.

"And we probably need to let these fumes dissipate," Garrett added, threading his fingers through Emilie's as they walked to the front of the coffee shop. "Give the stain a few days to finish drying. By next week, you can load those shelves to your heart's content."

"Thank you," she said again, every word heavy with her heartfelt appreciation.

"Like Jinx said, it was my pleasure," Garrett said with sincerity as he released her hand to wrap his arm across her shoulders and pull Emilie into his side. When they reached her side of the coffee counter, he kissed the top of her head before walking around to the customer stools, and again, Emilie wished for the ability to freeze time.

*A*lthough Emilie had not told a soul that Garrett would leave the next day, and she was certain he hadn't either, the entire coffee shop seemed to know...especially the seven nosy seniors holding court at the table in the far corner after lunch.

"He's really leaving?" Ms. Cheyenne asked, concern coloring her soft voice.

"Yes, ma'am," Emilie answered as she circled the table, topping off coffee cups.

"And you're just letting him go?" Alora Johnson asked.

"I can't force him to stay," Emilie replied.

"It's plain as day he's smitten with you," Blythe Asher cooed.

Obie nodded profusely, glee sparkling in his eyes.

"And it's plain to see you feel the same way," Mr. Sneed said with a sniffle.

Emilie felt like sniffling a little herself.

Of course she wanted him to stay...of course she'd fallen in love with the strong, steadfast, adorable, sweet and sexy hero.

"Perhaps he'll be back," Doc Ramon offered. "When the time is right." He smiled at Emilie with such encouragement and hope that her heart threatened to shatter even more.

"Or ask you to go," Alora said, almost on a challenge.

"*Pfff*," Mr. Moody groused. "Emilie belongs here."

"The two things may not be connected," Emilie told him with a raised eyebrow.

She left their table twittering about what *that* meant.

Emilie had slept little the night before.

She'd spent the hours juggling her sadness at the thought of Garrett leaving, her elation at their obvious feelings for one another, her uncertainty of what those two things meant for the future, and her worries about the future in general.

Jeremiah 29:11 came to mind and blanketed Emilie with peace: *"For I know the plans I have for you," declares the Lord, "plans to prosper you and not to harm you, plans to give you hope and a future."*

She would support whatever Garrett needed to do with patience and with faith that God had brought him into her life for a reason. She would have that talk with Mr. Moody, the one he'd avoided like the plague, and she'd finally make a plan to start her roastery...either in Green Hills or somewhere else. She was finished putting her professional life on hold. And she trusted in the Lord's plan.

That was all she could do.

Although doing so was easier said than done as the hours whittled away.

By closing time, her skin buzzed with anxiety over telling Garrett goodbye.

Her super seniors didn't help.

The last patrons to leave Brew, one by one, they approached Garrett on their way out.

"Thanks for the woodwork," Mr. Moody barked.

"And for all the help you gave Emilie with her holiday preparations," Doc Ramon added, extending his hand to shake Garrett's.

"Happy to do both," Garrett replied.

"I found an eagle feather on my porch this morning. They represent courage, leadership, and strength. I believe it is meant for you," Ms. Cheyenne explained, laying a long feather on his palm.

"It's exquisite," Garrett said, studying the intricate mottling pattern between the snow-white base and the smooth, dark-brown tip.

"Take care of yourself," Mr. Sneed instructed.

"Yes, sir, I will," Garrett promised.

"Write if you can," Alora suggested.

"Yes, ma'am," he agreed.

"For you," Blythe said, handing Garrett a quilted pillow, about fifteen inches square. "A piece of Green Hills to take with you wherever you go."

"I'll treasure it," he told her, admiring the stunning appliquéd depiction of his truck in front of Brew, decked out for Christmas, and a fetching woman behind the coffee counter.

Then Obie, who'd stood beside Garrett throughout the procession of farewells, took his turn, stepping to face Garrett. He gripped Garrett's hand in both his own, squeezing it tight. His tight lips forced a small smile as he looked deep into Garrett's eyes. After a long moment, perhaps a prayer, Obie — Marine veteran Obadiah Bernard — nodded his head, patted Garrett on the shoulder a few times, and then wiped tears from his cheeks as he walked away.

Emilie lost it.

A faint cry of despair escaped, and she turned to flee out the back. She couldn't do it; she couldn't take it. She didn't have it in her to say goodbye, not to him.

Garrett moved faster, closing his fingers around her wrist before she got away.

He pulled her into his arms and rocked Emilie while she cried.

"I don't leave until the morning," he said in a soothing voice. "We still have tonight."

In silent agreement, they cleaned up the coffee shop, turned off the lights, and locked the doors — side by side and clinging to one another every step.

Then Garrett followed Emilie home, where she parked her car and climbed into his truck. They drove to the Conrad Hotel, where Garrett packed his bags and checked out of his room.

"Turn here," Emilie said when Garrett pointed the truck toward her neighborhood. "I don't want to cook, and you can't leave town without trying Fish & Spoon."

That broke the ice of their quiet sorrow; they never stopped talking throughout dinner.

Garrett loved the fish and chips, and Emilie loved the brookie for dessert.

After dinner, Emilie directed Garrett to the marina at Daisy Lake, where — layered in coats and gloves and scarves — they huddled under a blanket in the bed of Garrett's truck to count stars and admire the lake, shimmering in moonlight.

Then they drove around Green Hills, listening to Christmas music on the radio while commenting about which houses had the best light displays and sharing what they loved most about the holidays.

When they got to Emilie's house, she mixed hot chocolate on the stove and Garrett built a fire in her cozy living room fireplace. They sipped their hot chocolate, snuggled in front of the fire, and talked well into the night.

Fighting to keep her eyes open, Emilie took Garrett's hand and led him to her bedroom.

Once there, she slid into her bathroom to change and brush her teeth.

Garrett grinned when she emerged in a one-piece, green-and-red-striped thermal union suit.

"I didn't want you to get the wrong idea," she told him, suddenly feeling shy.

"Emilie," he said, smoothing her hair back from her face to cup her jaw in his hands. "I know exactly who you are, and I just want to hold you for as long as I possibly can."

Happiness blossomed, radiating straight from her heart, through her veins, until it tingled in the tips of her fingers and toes. He did know her, just as she knew Garrett. She prayed someday they'd share more — share *everything*. She certainly wasn't immune to his rugged good looks, as the saying went. Like a magnet, her eyes went straight to him when he walked into a room. The way he looked at her made her pulse quicken. And her toes curled at the mere memory of that kiss they'd shared the night before. Garrett wanted her, too. Even a fool could tell that he did. Emilie was no fool…just a girl, crazy in love…with a man who had to leave.

She pushed that thought away and pushed him toward the bathroom.

While he was in there, Emilie moved the decorative pillows to the chair and pulled back the covers. She climbed in on her side and was sitting with her arms wrapped around her knees when he came back. She patted his side of the bed.

With a grin, he obeyed, sliding into her bed.

"This is nice," she said, scooting down and settling against Garrett's chest when he laid on his back. "New," she added as he wrapped his arms around her.

"A night I'll never forget," he said into her hair with a kiss.

Me neither.

It was her last conscious thought as she drifted off, cocooned in his warmth and counting the beats of his heart.

*E*milie awoke Friday morning feeling content and snuggly, but in an empty bed.

Garrett.

She knew without looking that he was gone.

But she looked over at his pillow. There lay a wooden angel. It had been whittled out of the same wood Garrett used on the shelving units. He'd left the figurine unstained, beautiful with raw warmth.

Emilie held it in her hand and brought her hand to her heart.

Part of her hated that he'd left without saying goodbye, but the other part was beyond grateful.

What was there to say?

He'd made a commitment to the Marines; more than that, in the fiber of his being, he *was* a Marine.

Garrett had to do what was right for *him.*

Just like Emilie needed to do what was right for her.

With a heavy heart, she went through her usual morning routine. Rehearsing what she planned to say to Mr. Moody kept her mind occupied, which helped.

The word *ultimatum* carried a negative connotation, which made the conversation she intended to force Mr. Moody into having more confrontational than she liked. But she'd been too sweet and too kind about Brew. She had a future there, or she didn't. It was that simple, and it was past time for Emilie to put her foot down and find out which it would be.

She waited to present her options until the morning crowd

had thinned and there were only a couple of tables occupied besides her seniors. She traded her Brew apron for a cropped tweed blazer. Emilie had ordered the tailored piece to have something whimsical yet still professional, and she loved the mossy and bronze colorway, so similar to a verdigris patina formed on copper. It looked great over the ruffled collar of her white oxford-style blouse and flowy chocolate-brown slacks. And if the army-green velvet loafers she'd paired with the outfit reminded her of the military, so be it. Garrett gave her strength. He'd believed in her and saw value in the vision she'd shared with him for the coffee shop and roastery. She'd use any and all reminders of him to bolster her confidence, which would prevent the memories from shattering her heart.

Emilie took a determined breath, squared her shoulders, and with file folder in hand, pulled up a chair to sit with her super seniors.

"Mr. Moody," she said, before anyone at the table could hijack the conversation. "Here is my two-week notice."

A blend of gasps sounded from six of the seven people as Emilie handed Mr. Moody a one-page resignation letter from her folder.

"And *this* is my offer to purchase Brew." She handed him the folder. "Inside you'll find a business proposal for us to work together over the next several years as I pay down your percentage of ownership. It includes proof of my financial qualifications and detailed plans for my vision and intentions for the coffee shop, which include purchasing the empty building next door and adding a small-batch roasting division to Brew. Finally, you'll find an envelope of napkin drawings, paint chips, fabric samples, lists, and illustrations of dreams for this place — *Roanna's* dreams." Emilie paused, letting him recover from that gut punch. "It was never her plan to let Brew sit and stagnate. Times you thought we were huddled together giggling or gossiping, we were brainstorming, tearing sheets from magazines and restaurant catalogs, and envisioning a grand future for this beautiful old building. I'm going to make our dreams come true, either here or somewhere else. You decide which."

Mic drop.

Emilie gave Mr. Moody a terse nod and then smiled at the other six retirees with a plea for assistance in her eyes, and went back to the storeroom, where she allowed three breaths to tremble with shaky nerves before switching her savvy blazer for her beloved Brew apron. Then she went back to work.

Mr. Moody eyed her with irritation when she took her place behind the coffee counter to serve a couple who'd arrived, but the rest of his companions twittered amongst themselves. Emilie strained to hear their words from across the dining room. Thankfully, with few patrons, it was quiet in there, and she could make out most of what they said.

Blythe and Obie were delighted. Blythe had commented that this meant Emilie would never leave Green Hills, and Obie had nodded with enthusiasm and his trademark smile.

Alora said something along the lines of, "That's a well-written presentation. She knows what she's doing…"

To which Mr. Sneed added, "She'll create something special. Alfy, she'll respect Roanna's part in the coffee shop's story. You can be sure of that."

"I'm not sure of anything," Mr. Moody argued. "This is still *my* coffee shop."

"This is *Roanna's* coffee shop," Ms. Cheyenne pointed out in a kind yet firm tone.

Mr. Moody turned a deeper shade of red.

"This is a good thing," Doc told him, setting a calming hand on Mr. Moody's wrist. "You never wanted to run this place. Cheyenne makes a good point: It *was* Roanna's baby. You were just supposed to be here sipping coffee while she had fun doing her thing during your retirement years. I'm sorry her illness robbed you both of that time together." Doc paused, and Mr. Sneed handed Mr. Moody a clean handkerchief from the breast pocket of his jacket. "Let Emilie take over Roanna's legacy. It's time."

At that, Emilie stepped into the kitchen to dry her own tears.

Leaving Brew, her town, and her precious seniors would crush her.

Please, Lord, don't make me do it. Open Mr. Moody's heart to leaving the shop in my care. I'll give it everything I have, God. You know I will. You put this dream on my heart, and I feel your hand in it. Give me faith that it will come true, Jesus. Give me faith. In your name, amen.

16

"Why, Grumpy, you do care."
Walt Disney's Snow White and the Seven Dwarfs
(1937)

Garrett considered driving all the way to the Marine Corps Base Quantico without stopping — except for gas and a snack when he absolutely had to. But his back wouldn't react well to eighteen uninterrupted hours in the truck, so he'd talked himself into breaking the drive into two stints.

Thoughts of Emilie consumed his mind during the first leg, from Green Hills to Nashville.

She'd been so beautiful, sleeping peacefully, her cheeks soft and warm, her lips peachy and begging to be kissed, and her silky blonde hair fanned across the pillow, tousled and wild. He'd remember that image until the day he died.

He wouldn't forget how much it hurt to leave her there, either.

But her life and her family and her world were in Green Hills, Oklahoma. It was where Garrett wanted to be, too. But it remained to be seen if that was an option, at least for the time being. And he wouldn't ask Emilie to wait. He didn't doubt that she'd have said she would. But that wasn't fair.

She'd have lived on hope for their future, insisting the love she didn't even try to hide from him was enough. And he'd have gone into every deployment, assignment, or mission with a niggling fear of her getting a call that he wasn't coming back, creating a weakness his team couldn't afford. He couldn't — *wouldn't* — do that to either of them.

Before he'd spent time in Green Hills — before meeting Emilie — Garrett had always assumed he'd retire from the Marines after thirty or forty years of active duty…or die on the job. The blast impact had challenged that assumption, but he'd been unable to see another life for himself. That was why he'd been desperate to find a way back to Tier 2 operating. Being a Marine Raider was all he knew.

But being in that homey little town, falling hard and fast for a gorgeous and spirited angel, and finishing that remodeling project with Jinx had opened Garrett's eyes to another way.

The first had been comforting, the second had happened quickly, but the third — his conversations with Jinx Malone — had really made the difference.

Their talks reminded Garrett that he knew things beyond being a soldier. Designing the new storeroom and working with his hands to complete it proved that he still had a knack for drafting and construction and that he enjoyed doing both… even more than he remembered.

Most of all, Jinx made Garrett see that changing one's course didn't mean he or she had failed on the first path. It was okay to develop a new plan and good — fun, even — to pursue a new dream.

He dreamed of Emilie.

In fact, she appeared in his dreams most nights. But the

night he spent in Nashville on his way back to base, the visions were especially vivid.

He saw them cheering in the stands at a football game, walking hand in hand at a Christmas tree lot, and kissing under the mistletoe. Then he saw them demoing the building next door to Brew, the one she wanted to transform into a small-batch roastery. In his sleep, he could smell the custom coffee blends she'd create. He also saw them working on the little cabins at Primrose Cottage, tearing out old fixtures and painting new walls. He envisioned a sketch of a vintage-styled roadside motel with a common courtyard and individual drives for each unit, an enticement to travelers on the highway leading into Green Hills.

That abandoned and dilapidated property had caught his attention. The prospect of turning it into something wonderful excited Garrett. He wanted it.

Not nearly in the same way he wanted Emilie, but he wanted to try… He wanted a life with her, tackling challenges, and embracing their community. Maybe some wedding bells and rugrats down the road.

That thought brought a big smile to Garrett's face as he exited I-95 to enter the base.

His online meeting with the Medical Evaluation Board a few days earlier had gone about how Garrett had expected. Given his training and experience, there were other jobs available to Garrett within the Corps, but they hadn't cleared him to return to full duty as an operator. The MEB had recommended up to twelve months of TLD — Temporary Limited Duty. He'd respectfully declined to wait another twelve months to see if his back got any better. The rods and pins in his spine weren't going anywhere; what did they think might change? So, they'd referred his case to the Physical Evaluation Board.

The PEB had called him back to headquarters to perform

its own assessment of his ability to serve. Garrett fully expected the PEB to assign a disability rating and suggest separation.

Physical disabilities. Unfit for service. Separation. Leave the Marines.

Fourteen years of training and deployments, work that made a person physically and mentally stronger than anyone thought they could be, and a gift that had saved an idiot teenager on a fast track to nowhere…it had become his calling, and it was all slipping away.

Garrett's stomach soured.

He provided credentials, parked on base, and carried his bag into the barracks they assigned to him.

At dinner in the chow hall, Garrett ran into a few Marines he knew and stayed a while to catch up with them. They talked him into walking over to the Hawkins Room for a drink or a cup of coffee. When he walked inside, the scent of Starbucks made him homesick for Brew.

He tried to be sociable, but his heart wasn't in it. His heart was in Green Hills with Emilie.

Claiming a long day of driving and an early report time in the morning — both of which were true — Garrett left his buddies after an hour and went back to his apartment-style room. There he washed up, sliding on a Brew T-shirt he'd bought as a keepsake…just in case he didn't get back. It smelled like the coffee shop with a hint of Emilie's spicy perfume. Funny how scents could cover one in peace.

Garrett piled pillows against the headboard and opened his laptop to do some research. He found the property records for the land and improvements included in the Primrose Cottages parcel and plugged the tax figures into a new spreadsheet. Next, he searched for historical roadside motels of the mid-1900s. The history fascinated Garrett. The accessibility of family vehicles had led to road trips and vacations. Those had established a need for overnight lodgings at reasonable prices. Then, the initiative to improve roads and create interstate highways made the roadside motels obsolete. As history exists within a continuous cycle, families were once again embracing holiday trips off the beaten path. They were making time for small-town excursions and finding innovative places to explore. Other people had seen the same potential and opportunity he did, which had prompted a resurgence of renovated — often themed — properties.

Maybe this idea isn't so crazy after all.

At midnight, Garrett forced himself to stop imagining the *what-ifs*. But before he closed the laptop, he opened another browser window to start a search on small-batch coffee roasteries. He had a lot to learn.

Garrett also opened his email app and started a message to his dad. It was time to reach out. No matter what happened over the next few days of medical appointments and hearings, his life was about to change. He'd proven he wasn't the screw-up his dad remembered and loathed. Garrett had served his country well; he'd protected and saved and even killed for freedom. He had nothing to feel ashamed of anymore. He could face his father, and he needed to, needed to heal that wound so he could start fresh and feel whole.

Emilie made him believe he was whole, not a useless, broken soldier.

He pulled the T-shirt over his head and balled it up on his pillow. Then he turned off the lamp, inhaled her scent, and went to sleep thinking of his angel.

*I*t turned out the next few days went *exactly* as Garrett had suspected they would: lots of grueling exams, tiresome interviews, and too much poking and prodding. He'd aced the mental exercises, failed most of the physical ones, gritted his teeth through the interviews, and tolerated the doctors.

Although far stronger than a typical civilian, Garrett couldn't pass the rigorous certification requirements for elite forces. On the bright side, the findings did not show that his "impairments would reduce the Marine's ability to engage in gainful employment or normal activity" outside the military.

How they handled his future was completely up to the PEB and the SECNAV representative sent by the Secretary of the Navy.

"You are three years into a five-year enlistment contract," the woman began, without an introduction or preamble or *How's it going?*

"Yes, ma'am," Garrett confirmed, sitting ramrod straight in his chair, feeling like a Marine in the uniform but not in his own skin.

"And you've declined another period of TLD?"

"Yes, ma'am," he answered again.

"Are you interested in other areas of service besides combat operations? Your aptitude and intelligence tests show a strong inclination for logistics; you'd do well in campaign support and event management."

"With all due respect to those reports, ma'am, and despite what my brain might have indicated on paper, I'm not cut out for a desk job, and I don't see myself throwing Marine Birthday Balls."

She frowned at Garrett's obvious lack of respect for jobs *someone* had to do. He didn't doubt they did them really well. It just wouldn't be Garrett doing them.

"Could you see your way to assisting in those capacities if a need arises?"

Garrett eyed her suspiciously.

"*If?*" he asked. "Or *when?* And for how long?"

She pursed her lips, apparently not impressed he'd seen

right through her ploy. Garrett wasn't about to agree to something vague and indefinite. If he couldn't kick down doors, he was going home to Emilie, and the sooner the better.

"SECNAV reviewed your service history personally," she said. That got Garrett's attention. "You've been quite an asset to the country these past fourteen years," she added. The grateful look in her eyes humbled him.

"Thank you, ma'am."

"Which means you are six years away from full retirement. SECNAV likes to see our soldiers benefit from their service for the rest of their lives. We want that for you, too."

Six more years? Behind a desk or planning parties?

"I'm sorry, ma'am—"

"So we're putting you on IRR," she said over him.

Independent Ready Reserve? For six years?

"You'll attend IRR Administrative Muster training once a year and perform various administrative obligations from time to time, mostly attending ceremonial functions — but *not* planning them," she added with a look of disdain at how he'd referred to that particular assignment. "At fulfillment of your current Military Service Obligation, you'll be eligible to retire with full benefits. And throughout your time on IRR, you'll continue with mandated medical care, necessary procedures, and therapy to minimize the chronic effects of injuries sustained in combat."

Garrett eyed the form she slid to his side of the table.

This is it.

An exit strategy removing him from all he'd ever been.

His heart raced. His knee wanted to bounce with energy, but he'd been trained to control his reactions in all situations. So he simply stared at it.

You're not that anymore anyway. Sign the paper, his conscience screamed in his head.

Garrett took the pen she offered.

It felt like signing a confession: *I, Gunnery Sergeant Garrett James Banks, admit I'm broken and no longer any good to my unit or my country. And because I'm useless, I'll take this deal and disappear so as not to embarrass the Corps that I love.*

"While I understand this is difficult," the SECNAV rep said, her voice much more empathetic than it had been moments earlier, "it *is* a win-win — for the Marine Corps, which values your input and representation; your country, which wishes to honor you; and your family, who I'm sure wants you to continue healing and moving forward. You are a hero to us all; nothing will ever change that."

Family. Emilie. She knows only the broken me. Somehow, she loves me all the same.

With a vision of her smile in his mind, Garrett signed the paper removing himself from active duty, Tier 2 operating, and his life as a Marine Raider.

Less than twenty minutes later, he was on the road to Oklahoma.

He'd been gone six days, but it felt like six months.

Needing to hear her voice, he called the coffee shop before it closed.

"Brew…this is Juni; can I take your order?"

"*Juni?*" he asked, completely confused by the singsong greeting. Who was Juni?

"That's me. You know, just like Junie B. Jones," a bubbly, youthful voice laughed. "Do you want something?"

More like someone.

"Is Emilie there?"

"Nope," Juni answered.

"When do you expect her back?" he asked, desperate for better intel.

"I dunno."

"Do you know where she went?" Garrett reminded himself to stay calm; growling at the flighty-sounding teenager wouldn't help, even if it would make him feel a whole lot better.

"Mrs. Asher, Doc…any of y'all know where Emilie went? Some guy on the phone wants to know," Juni yelled into the restaurant.

Then Juni must've dropped the phone because all Garrett heard was a series of thumps followed by garbled, distant voices.

"This is Doctor Alden Ramon; may we help you?"

Finally, someone with some sense.

"Doc, it's Garrett. I was hoping to talk to Emilie."

Nothing but silence.

"Doc? You still there? It's Garrett Banks. Remember?"

"Of course, son. I was just…*uh*…relaying something to the table."

Garrett grinned. Nosey old busybodies. He shook his head, because Emilie sure loved them.

"Do you know where Emilie is?" Garrett tried again.

"Yes, well, it's not really our news to tell," he said, hemming and hawing.

Garrett heard muffled hollering in the background.

Then another shuffling of the phone.

"This is Alora Johnson. Why are you calling our Emilie?"

"Well, that's not really your news to know," he said, tossing their own argument right back at Emilie's meddlesome seniors.

"I'll tell you, if you'll tell me." She dangled her proposal in the air.

"Deal," Garrett replied. "I'm driving as fast as the law allows from the Commonwealth of Virginia to Green Hills, Oklahoma, to make Emilie mine. Forever."

"*Woo-wee*," Alora squealed, right in Garrett's ear.

"But don't tell her!" he added, praying he could get there fast enough, knowing good and well his secret wouldn't stay safe for long.

"She's not here to tell anyhow," Alora said, testing Garrett's patience. "She and Alfy are at the lawyer's office. He's finally signing over Brew. The coffee shop is gonna be Emilie's — *officially*."

Garrett's heart soared for Emilie.

Thank you, God, for making that happen.

The praise popped into his mind of its own accord, but Garrett didn't mind. Either Emilie's faith had rubbed off on him a little, or she'd helped him rediscover a peace so deep it reopened his heart to having a relationship with the Lord. Probably, it had been a bit of both. Either way, good memories from attending church as a child were coming back to him, and Garrett found that talking to God got easier and easier the more he did it.

"Alora? Are you still there?"

"I'm here," she answered. "But when will *you* be here?"

"Soon. It's a long drive, but I'll be there soon. Can you all keep it quiet until I arrive? I'd like to surprise Emilie. Please?"

Alora must've covered the phone with her hand because Garrett couldn't hear the discussion on the other end of the line. But his spirits soared when she returned, announcing, "We're in!"

17

Coffee, the favorite drink of the civilized world.
Thomas Jefferson

Garrett pulled into Green Hills at 10:00 a.m. on Christmas Eve.

Ignoring the sharp pangs in his back, he'd driven all the way from Quantico. Taking a few minutes to walk when he stopped for food and gas every four hours had helped, but it still took a second to ease from his truck and limp his way into Brew…

Only to be greeted by a bouncy brunette with a ponytail that swayed like a clock's pendulum, one who looked like she was about twelve years old. Since employment laws required workers to be at least sixteen, Garrett guessed that was Juni.

Lord, give me patience.

"Morning," he said, making his way to his favorite stool at the counter and trying to sound less like someone who'd stayed up all night and desperately needed a cup of coffee. And his angel.

"Merry *almost* Christmas," she said with cheerful exuberance.

Ah, to be young.

At the moment, Garrett felt ninety-two instead of thirty-two. No wonder the United States government had deemed him unfit for service.

"I'd love a cup of coffee." He practically groaned sitting down on the stool.

"You bet," she said, head bobbing with a big smile. Garrett could totally see her being a Wolf Pack cheerleader. "Anything in it?"

"Just black. Thanks," he added when she filled a mug in front of him. "It's pretty quiet in here today." Even the big round table in the front corner was empty.

"Everyone's at the festival." Juni's big eyelashes blinked at him as though he'd grown a second head.

"I bet you'd rather be there, too." Garrett sipped his coffee, giving the girl plenty of space to talk.

And she did.

"Yes, but I'm brand-new…just started working here Monday, so I'm stuck manning the coffee shop until the owner gets back this afternoon."

New owner or old owner?

"Then I have to go help with our coffee stand at the festival, but she promised I'll still have time to shop with my friends," Juni continued.

Bingo…new owner.

"I *really* didn't want a job right now," the teenager bemoaned. "But I accidentally tapped Mrs. Crockett's bumper at a red light — I mean, it hardly did any damage at all. But I *might* have been looking at my phone when she stopped in front of me *very suddenly*, without any warning at all. So my parents were, like, really mad at me. And my grandma is good friends with Mrs. Crockett, who's married to the police chief. Anyway, she told Grandma I was on my phone when it happened, and Chief Crockett said I was responsible for fixing his wife's car. So now I'm expected to come up with *four thousand, seven hundred thirty-eight dollars and sixty-two cents!*"

Not quite what Garrett would term *hardly any damage at all.*

He *hemmed* consolingly, and she kept rolling.

"One of my brothers — I have four of them — went to school with Jax Fielding, who is fixing Mrs. Crockett's car. Well, Jax told my brother that his sister needed to hire seasonal help at Brew. Now I have to work all through Christmas break and around our cheerleading schedule until I pay off my debt to society." Juni rolled her eyes dramatically, and Garrett bit his lip to keep from laughing at her predicament.

"I miss hanging out with my friends," she said with a huff. "But Emilie's super cool, and she said this'll look good on my resume for when I want a part-time job in college because there are *tons* of trendy coffee shops around college campuses. She also said the cutest boys hang out in coffee shops, so you just never know who you might meet at work."

Did she now?

Then Juni smiled flirtatiously at Garrett, prompting him to get out of there quickly. The loquacious girl kept talking while he snatched a few dollars from his wallet, took the last drink of his coffee, and set the money under the mug.

"Plus, Emilie already paid her brother what I owe him for fixing Mrs. Crockett's car. That was awfully sweet of her. But she said we all need a helping hand at times, so someday I'll need to pay it forward for someone else. Emilie's really smart, too. And pretty! I want to be just like her when I'm old," Juni added with a fanciful sigh.

Garrett didn't have the heart to tell Juni that Emilie was only twenty-eight, and he couldn't argue with the pretty part. In fact, he was champing at the bit to see that beautiful face with his own two eyes.

"Thanks," he told Emilie's effusive new employee, but she'd already moved down the counter to talk the ear off another poor soul who'd wandered into the shop.

Garrett started his truck, put it in gear, and then hesitated.

It sounded like Emilie had her hands full for a few more hours. He was happy to go help her, but he also wanted Emilie to himself when she found out he'd returned. Add to that, he'd been awake for almost twenty-nine hours and could use some sleep.

He pointed his truck toward the Conrad Hotel, expecting to rent another room, but the streets all around the hotel were closed for the festival. The detour sent him on a path toward Emilie's house.

She'd said, *You're always welcome here.* Garrett was going to find out if she meant it.

He smiled with satisfaction when the code he'd set still worked.

Then, he carried in his duffel bag and went to her room to borrow the shower.

Everything smelled like Emilie…the soap, the shampoo, the towels. Garrett decided that drowning in her scent wouldn't be a bad way to go.

After he'd dressed in sweatpants and an undershirt, he set an alarm on his phone before stretching out on the couch to nap for a while.

Garrett felt like a new human when his phone chimed at four o'clock.

Quickly, he changed into boots, jeans, and a pullover sweater. Then he stopped by the flower shop for two bouquets: one of roses and one of mistletoe. He asked the florist to wrap both of them in boxes, so Emilie couldn't see inside.

He arrived at Brew at 4:30, just as Emilie began switching off the lights in the dining room to close up for the day. She stood behind the counter fiddling around the cash register when he pushed open the door.

The bells above it jingled, but she didn't look up. Garrett stepped into the dining room and set the flower boxes on a table.

"So sorry," she said, still hunting for whatever she sought. "We're out of coffee for today."

"I'm not here for coffee this time."

Emilie's head snapped up, with hope and love and joy shining in her eyes.

He smiled back, and she flew around the counter and practically jumped through the air, wrapping her arms around his neck with forceful meaning.

Garrett circled his arms around her, matching the strength of her happiness and burying his face in the soft silkiness of her hair.

God, she feels good. Please, Lord, never take her away.

When Garrett set Emilie back on her feet, she dried tears from her face and looked up at him like he was the best thing she'd ever seen.

They couldn't stop smiling at one another.

"Here," he said. "Pick a box."

"Any box?" she teased.

Garrett balanced one on each palm.

Emilie chose the opposite hand she'd selected when he'd played that game with her key to the coffee shop, just as he'd predicted she would.

He held out the box for her to open.

She lifted the Christmas-themed bouquet, arranged with red roses, white lilies, evergreen sprigs, and holly berries. A thick, red velvet ribbon, the exact color of Santa's suit, held the fragrant elements together with a perfect bow.

"They're beautiful," Emilie gasped, inhaling the sweet scent of the flowers and closing her eyes in bliss.

"*You're* beautiful," Garrett corrected.

"Thank you," she said, her voice heavy with sincerity and something he couldn't quite name but felt in equal measure, like an intangible truth that they'd never get enough of one another. "And what's in the other box?" she asked.

"That one's for me," he told her with a sly wink. "All done closing the shop?"

"I guess," Emilie answered. "I asked Juni, my new helper—"

"Oh, I know Juni," Garrett said, interrupting with wry humor.

"Do you now? Well, do you know where she left the list of high school volunteers who signed up to help at the coffee booth?"

"I'd imagine she doesn't know where she left it either."

"She *is* a little scattered," Emilie said with indulgent patience. "She's a good kid, though — just young. And with four older brothers, she's been pretty sheltered and extremely pampered."

"It sounds like you've taken her under your wing…given her sound advice about a few things."

"Oh really? Like what?"

"Like meeting cute boys in coffee shops," Garrett bragged.

"Well, of course." Emilie agreed too hastily. "I've met *loads* of them. They come in all the time. I can barely keep up with their names; there are so many to choose from—"

Garrett swooped in and cut her off with a kiss.

While he kissed her, Emilie set her flowers on the closest table and wrapped her arms back around his neck, threading her fingers into his hair and pulling him closer.

When he lifted his head to look into her eyes, they were both struggling to catch their breath.

"How many?" he asked, voice husky and low.

"Just one." Her confession filled his heart.

"You sure?"

"I'm all yours for as long as you want me," Emilie pledged.

"Forever sounds good to me."

"Forever?" she asked, sounding scared to believe what she'd heard.

"I'd like to stick around this time, if that's okay." Garrett traced a finger down her cheek, his eyes following the caress.

"But— You were in your uniform. And then you left. I thought…" Emilie trailed off.

"Driving away from Green Hills — from you — was one of the most difficult things I've ever done. I couldn't get back fast enough. But I was called to base; not going was not an option."

"Why didn't you tell me?"

"Because I wasn't sure how things would go."

"How *did* they go?" Emilie asked. Worry waged with hope in her eyes.

"Good," Garrett said with a grin. "That is, if you don't mind my hanging around for a while."

"For *forever?*" She echoed his earlier promise with more conviction.

"If you'll have me." His heart threatened to beat out of his chest.

"Just until the end of time," Emilie vowed. Then she took hold of the lapels of his jacket and pulled his lips down to hers, sealing the deal with a kiss.

"Can we go home?" Garrett asked, nibbling his way down the soft skin along the side of her neck.

He felt more than heard her purr.

But then she burst his bubble…

"I have to go back to the festival," she told him. "I'm in charge of the tree lighting ceremony tonight."

Garrett rested his forehead against hers, fighting the urge to see just how tempting he could be.

But if anyone understood and respected one's commitment to their word, it was Garrett Banks.

"Will there be anything to eat at the festival?" he asked.

"Ha! *Will there be anything to eat?* I hope you're hungry," she teased. Then she began listing all the options while locking up the coffee shop.

Hand in hand and leaning into one another, they walked to the courthouse square where, besides restaurants open late, a multitude of food trucks and vendors offered every style of cuisine Garrett could want. Surrounded by the delicious aromas from food booths, artisans, crafters, woodworkers, and owners of local boutiques displayed their wares. On a nearby stage, a band played holiday tunes while couples danced and children played.

"I thought these things were just in the movies," Garrett said, amazed by one thing after another. "It's like a Norman Rockwell Christmas print come to life."

"You'll get used to it," Emilie said with a hint of pride. She never hid how much she adored her charming hometown.

"I don't think it'll take long," he agreed.

When Emilie went to meet the rest of her committee members, Garrett did a little shopping and some exploring. He'd just discovered a booth selling impressive handmade wooden furniture when a familiar voice called his name.

"You're back," Jinx Malone stated, a knowing glint in his eyes.

"I'm back," Garrett agreed with a guilty grin. "They offered a solution that benefited us both — me more than the Marines, but who am I to protest their plan?"

"They are the United States government," Jinx teased.

"These yours?" Garrett asked, pointing toward the furniture pieces.

"Hopefully not for long."

"You just do furniture?"

"What do you have in mind?" Jinx asked, answering Garrett's question with one of his own.

"I'm thinking about taking on another remodel project."

"More work at the coffee shop?"

"Emilie might have some projects I'll help with now that she owns Brew, but I'm looking at something else, something that'll need a lot of framing and craftsmanship."

"I'm intrigued," Jinx said with a nod. "And I can hook you up with experts for the parts that aren't my specialty."

"I'd appreciate that," Garrett said at the same time the band finished on stage and Emilie's voice drifted over the sound system. "I'll be in touch."

"You know where to find me," Jinx said. "I'm glad you're back," he added.

"Me too," Garrett replied as he turned to walk toward the massive Christmas tree waiting to shine.

He watched, and he listened…to the people, the camaraderie, the community. It was a new way of life, but one that fit, like he'd been destined to be there all along, when the time was right.

Emilie stood on stage, talking and laughing with friends she'd known most of her life. Her bright-blonde hair blew around her shoulders under a knit beanie, and she bounced up and down trying to stay warm. She was so gorgeous, so energetic and vivacious. Just looking at her made his chest tighten.

She met his gaze and waved, rubbing her arms and pantomiming, *It's sooo cold out here!*

Garrett couldn't wait to get her home…knew exactly how to warm her up.

18

Snow White: Once there was a princess…
Doc: Was the princess you?
Snow White: And she fell in love.
Sneezy: Was it hard to do?
Snow White: It was very easy. Anyone could see
that the Prince was charming.
The only one for me.
Doc: Was he strong and handsome?
Sneezy: Was he big and tall?
Snow White: There's nobody like him,
anywhere at all.
Bashful: Did he say he loved ya?
Happy: Did he steal a kiss?
Snow White [singing]: He was so romantic…
I could not resist.
Dialog and lyrics from
"Someday My Prince Will Come"
in Disney's Snow White and the Seven Dwarfs (1937)

*A*s promised, at least to himself, Garrett had held and snuggled and cuddled with Emilie — with a few heated kisses mixed in — until she'd defrosted, relaxed, and eventually fallen asleep in his arms. He intended for them to fall asleep just that way, every single night.

When he woke before her on Christmas morning, Garrett covered her with an extra quilt and crept out of her room without making a noise. Then he opened the flower box full of mistletoe and ribbon, which he'd asked the florist to toss in. It took a minute to find a pair of scissors, so by the time he began hanging clusters of mistletoe all over Emilie's house, he worried she'd catch him in the act.

Garrett watched his back as if he were on a covert mission. He'd just hung the last mini bouquet and tucked one of his presents into his pocket and the rest under the tree when he heard her bedroom door open. Hopping over the couch and grabbing a Christmas book from the lamp table, he looked like the picture of innocence when she came down the hall.

"Merry Christmas," he said as her eyes scanned the blooms overtaking her house.

"What is this?" she asked, eyes wide with wonder.

"I didn't want you to get the wrong idea," he told her, holding out his hand for her to clasp.

She giggled and put her hand in his. Garrett pulled her around the couch and lowered Emilie onto his lap.

"And what is the *right* idea?" she asked, smiling as she wrapped her arms around his neck and shoulders.

"That this is real," Garrett told her. His tone had switched to one more serious, one that left no doubt of his sincerity. "I love you. I'm *in* love with you," he clarified. "And I want to spend the rest of my life showing you how much. This happened quickly, Emilie, but it doesn't make it any less real for me. This is right."

"Garrett—" Emilie started to speak, then changed her mind. Grabbing his face, she held it in front of hers, searching his eyes. He let her see exactly how he felt about her. She leaned in and brushed her lips across his, then nipped at his mouth, taking control and deepening the kiss at her own pace. Patience tested his willpower, but for Emilie to believe in his love, he could withstand anything, even the most perfect form of torture.

"You love me?" she asked.

"Yes."

"You want to make a life with me?"

"Yes."

"And you're sure?"

"Yes."

"Don't joke."

"Never about this. You're my future, where I belong."

"This is what you really want?"

"*You* are what I want."

"And you're sure?" she asked again.

Garrett chuckled, smiling at the hope so evident in her glassy eyes.

"More than I've ever been about anything in my entire life," he said, placing his hands over hers, which were still framing his face. He guided them to his lips, kissing one of her palms and then the other. Then, he stacked her hands in his, reached into his pocket and retrieved her gift, a marquise-cut diamond set on a vintage gold band. He'd seen it in the case at the antique shop on the square and known it was meant for Emilie.

"You're mine," he said. "And I'm yours. This is so you don't forget." He slid the ring on her finger and looked up to meet her gaze. "When you're ready to call it an engagement, you let me know." Garrett swiped the tears on her cheeks with his thumbs and indulged in a quick kiss on her lips. "And when you're ready to walk down the aisle, you tell me when and where, and I'll be there."

Emilie launched herself at him, trying her best to squeeze the life out of him by strangling his neck with exuberance. "I love you," she said. "I love you, I love you, I love you," she repeated again and again. Then she planted kisses all over his face, unrelenting until he started laughing, unable to hold back his happiness. "You're stuck with me," she warned. "Forever. Now that you're home, I'll never let you go."

The bossy glint in her eyes thrilled Garrett.

"*You are my home.* There's nowhere else I want to be," he told her, proving his claim with another searing kiss.

"I hope you have a lot more of those," Emilie taunted.

"Kisses?" Garrett asked.

"Yes, I hope you're up for *a lot* of kissing… Someone turned our house into a mistletoe farm," she teased.

"That they did," he agreed with pride, leaning in to prove his abilities.

That they did.

* * *

At Christmas, all roads lead home.
Marjorie Holmes

* * *

he End.

GREEN HILLS BOOK 8 PLAYLIST

***Music can change the world
because it can change people.
Bono***

Enjoy the music that helped inspire the story…

1. Soldier, Poet, King - The Oh Hellos
2. Christmas Wish - Katherine McNamara
3. That Holiday Feelin' - Mr & Mrs
4. Catch Me (I'm Falling) - Pretty Poison
5. Christmas Kiss - Tatum Sheets
6. Soldier - James TW
7. Christmas Kisses - Serena Ryder
8. Merry & Bright - ARZA
9. What Child Is This - Bing Crosby
10. Christmas Kisses - Ray Anthony
11. Soldier Boy - The Shirelles
12. Carrying Your Love With Me - George Strait
13. Soldier - Fleurie and Tommy Profitt
14. A Change Is Gonna Come - Sam Cooke

15. I Choose Love - Shawn Gallaway
16. Some Day My Prince Will Come - Adriana Caselotti
17. Here's My Home - Alex Cap
18. Christmas Kiss - Meaghan Smith

———

Available on Spotify as
"Book 8: A Hero's Christmas Kiss
by Virginia'dele Smith"

ABOUT THE AUTHOR

Ashli Montgomery is a wife, a momma, a writer, a quilter, and an entrepreneur. Her passion is sharing love stories, books, quilts, yoga, recipes, her faith, and her favorite ways to create a lovely life.

She is quilting to mend the mind by spearheading a community of quilters through Quilt 2 End ALZ, Inc., a 501(c)(3) nonprofit she launched to use her quilting hobby as a platform to advocate for an end to Alzheimer's disease.

Ashli writes wholesome and cozy romance under the pen name *Virginia'dele Smith* to honor Syble Virginia Tidwell, Adele Gertrude Baylin, and Etta Jean Smith.

These three cherished grandmothers taught Ashli to love without judgment, always putting family first. Through Grandma Syble's journals and appetite for books, through Momadele's priceless cards and handwritten letters, and through hours of visiting over fabric at Mema's kitchen island, Ashli also learned to treasure words.

Get to know Ashli by subscribing to her newsletter, *The Gazette*, at AshliMontgomery.com

Titles by Virginia'dele Smith

Sadie & Sam: PART 1 - Introductory Short Story (FREE)
Book 0: My Manifesto - Short Memoir (FREE)

The Davenports
Book 1: Grocery Girl
Book 2: In the Trenches
Book 3: Three Times to Make Sure
Book 4: Take a Chance on Love
The Davenports EAT — A Green Hills Cookbook

Book 5: Undeveloped Love
A Christmas Collection Novella

Book 6: Stealing Kisses
A Valentine's Sweetheart Story

Book 7: Phoebe
A Green Hills Historical Romance and The Prairie Roses Collection #50

Picture of Love
A Green Hills Short Story Featured in The Pumpkin Spice Romance anthology

Book 8: A Hero's Christmas Kiss
A Christmas Collection Novella and part of the Military Kisses Sweet Romance series

The Green Hills of Scotland (coming soon)
Book 9: Isla
Book 10: Ainslie
Book 11: Elspeth

***Ashli not only writes about
quilts, quilters, and quilting…
She's a quilter, too!***

When she's not writing, Ashli is often helping others complete their quilt projects through her longarm sewing business, Longarm Lucey, and *quilting to mend the mind* by connecting quilters with the fight to end Alzheimer's disease through Quilt 2 End ALZ, Inc., a 501(c)(3) nonprofit she launched in 2019, to use her quilting hobby as a platform to advocate for a world without Alzheimer's disease and other forms of dementia. Learn more at Quilt2EndALZ.org 🩶